THE FORCE OF LIFE'S CONFESSIONS

Order this book online at www.trafford.com
or email orders@trafford.com

Most Trafford titles are also available at major online book retailers.

Note for Librarians: A cataloguing record for this book is available from Library
and Archives Canada at www.collectionscanada.ca/amicus/index-e.html

Printed in Victoria, BC, Canada.

ISBN: 978-1-4269-1011-1 (sc)
ISBN: 978-1-4269-1013-5 (e)

*Our mission is to efficiently provide the world's finest, most comprehensive book publishing
service, enabling every author to experience success. To find out how to publish your book, your
way, and have it available worldwide, visit us online at www.trafford.com*

Trafford rev. 9/2/2009

www.trafford.com

North America & international
toll-free: 1 888 232 4444 (USA & Canada)
phone: 250 383 6864 ♦ fax: 812 355 4082

DEDICATION

To My family and friends for through you all was a dim light made brighter. Special Thanks to my advisor through which all my strength was provided. Thank you Father God.

This book has been written in memory of My Father Marion Pinckney, My Mother and Father-in-Law Loretta Young-Whitaker and Dennis Maybin.
To Darla Rodriquez fly away my angel.
May you all rest in peace.

ACKNOWLEDGEMENTS

I would like to give special thanks: To God, for all the blessings he has bestowed upon me; Dale Maybin my husband for being supportive of my choice to become a writer; Elaunte, Elaundre, and Tamika Foster my children for understanding and loving me unconditionally; Rosetta (Alexander) Clifford my mother and stepfather for encouraging me to become more and work hard for everything; Tammy and Louis Graham my second parents for teaching me the importance of moral values and the content of character; Marion Pinckney J.R, Earth Moore, Charles Pinckney, Isaac McMillan, Marvina Pinckney, Vera Moore, Albertina Sherrod, Ellen Sherrod, Verstine Johnson, Darrell Griffin, Rosemae Harris, Darren McMillan, Rodney McMillan, Brittany Jossirin, and Lamille Jossirin my siblings for being apart of my life and helping to shape me into the person I have become today; Kimberly Davis, Margret Babb-Wells, Marlo Ferguson, Tracy Tolbert, Krisandra Thompson, and Darla Rodriquez, my (sisters)and best friends for always supporting my dreams; The McMillan Family, Johnson Family, Perry Family, Moore Family, Maybin Family, Digg Family, Campbell Family, Young Family and Pinckney Family for without you my life would not be complete; To my church family at Mt. Sinai Missionary Baptist Church of Fort Myers, Florida, To Pastor Dr. Benny Mcleod, Cynthia Mcleod, Shelia Pearsey, The Women of Gospel, and The Junior Women Auxillery of Mt. Sinai thank you so much for blessing me with your love, compassion and inspiration to continue putting God first. Thank you to my entire family, my friends and colleagues for encouraging me to keep writing, for providing feedback, and most importantly for your love and support. For with any progress and productivity in which I have; I share with you all for I could not have done it without you. I love you and may God bless you all.

A special thanks to Sharnice Brown, Corrine Goree, Clarissa McCoy-Person, Tamarish Smith, Sarah Damico and Stephen Moore (The models used for photos in this book) Models for this book are merely models and in no way does this book depict the lives of any persons photographed.

The characters in this story are fictional and in no way do the lives of these characters reflect the real life story of anyone. Any similarities are coincidental.

CHAPTER 1

"Hey Stephanie, wait up girl!" Dang you walk fast. Stephanie was on a mission, she had to meet Roger before he went to class. Roger was a worry wart and he would have a panic attack whenever she was late. "Hey Step are we still on for tonight, Kim asked?" "Oh Yeah for sure," says Stephanie. "Alright girl, I will catch you later," said Kim as they parted. Stephanie was going to borrow her mother's car so they could all go and hang out on their last night as high school juniors. It was the end of the school year and they were all setting out to make waves in their very small yet, tight knit circle of friends for the upcoming year as seniors. Stephanie, Naomi, Lucy who they called La La,

Mia, and Kim had all been friends since grammar school. They had spent most of their lives together and they were more like sisters then friends. Later that evening they made plans to drive around the west side of Delray City. While riding around in Stephanie mother's two toned 1984 Ford station wagon the girls prepared themselves to make their rounds in the local neighborhood projects. Although their means of transportation wasn't anything to sneeze at it was all they needed to experience the will to be free from the glaring eyes of their parents on the weekend. Stephanie mother's car was huge, with enough room for the entire girls' basketball team. The car was covered in dark grey primer with what was left of its original hot pink paint job. The car had two thick white wall tires on the front and two oversized tires on the back. Every time the car hit a pot hole or bump it would bounce high enough to give the girls that queasy feeling in the pit of their stomach; like the feeling they would get from the rides at the county fair. Stephanie's mother always kept her crushed aluminum cans in the rear of the car. The girls would often tease Stephanie about her mother's eccentric hobby. Stephanie would always defended her mother's right to collect aluminum cans by stating; "*My mother is doing her part to help preserve the earth through recycling."* Stephanie's mother also had a very distasteful set of pink and black dice hanging from the mirror. Despite Mrs. Strom's poor designer taste for her car, she was very eloquent, classy and had great fashion sense when it came to all her other material possessions. Her station wagon was one of four family owned cars which she seldom used. The car had been in the family for over twenty years. Mrs. Strom considered it to be a family heirloom since it was the last of her father's material possession in which she owned after he passed away sixteen years ago. During their weekend excursion the girls were all dressed to impress. The girls took pride in their ability to dress in the latest fashions'. While planning and plotting earlier that evening they had foreseen a future of finding an interesting hangout to acquire social stimulating conversations about the next year's popularity contest. The girl's weekend ritual consisted of them all chipping in for gas and food. They had devised this plan because it was a lot cheaper and it allowed them to have money available for the next weekend's excursion just in case their parents felt the need to deduct from their allowance due to some unforeseen error they would make such as over extending themselves at the mall. Although the girls were social bunnies they were economically gifted. As they listened to Luther Vandross's *"Here and Now"* on the radio they fixed their makeup, hair and were ready to hit the scene. They wanted to make sure they were well put together before driving through the west side projects. As they drove up to the light on 47th and Manny Terrace they could see the lights on the courts. Stephanie pulled up to the courts and parked. There was always a gang of college guys playing basketball on the courts because it was so close to Delray University. Stephanie, Lucy and Naomi were the first to exit the car. The girls begin gossiping while looking at the guys and laughing loud enough to get the guys attention as they exited the car. They sat on the top of the car and watched as the guys who were much older and sophisticated shoot hoops. As Kim and Mia joined the other girls they all pretended to be too engrossed in their own conversation to notice when the guys stopped briefly to gawk at them. Stephanie was the only one of the girls who truly ignored the guy's advances for she was Roger's girl. Roger and Stephanie had been together since middle school and they were as she loves to coin as her own personal phrase, *"laying and staying together for life"*. As Kim stood watching Stephanie blow kisses to Roger through the fence she pondered how she could never really understand how Stephanie was willing to sacrifice her future and her soul by giving up her precious temple to Roger so frequently. After discussing all the drama that happen in school the girls decided to walk closer to the courts and sit on the bleachers. As they all walked along the fence on their way to the bleachers they played their ritual of cat and mouse with the guys. They would yell through the fence talking to the guys and then when the guys eagerly responded to their playful advances the girls would then pretend not to hear them. They would look at the guys just long enough to let them know they were interested; as soon as the guys responded or made advances to this behavior they would turn away. As they walked along the fence Kim began to ponder the lives of her friends and her very own. Stephanie although she was proclaimed by Roger received the most attention whenever the girls went out. She was 5'9 145 lbs with a 24 inch waistline and hips that were the size of Christmas hams. She was the daughter Mr. and Mrs. Strom A.K.A Mr. and Mrs. Neighborhood Watch. Stephanie was very strong minded, determined and the leader in the group. She seemed to be the only one of them who was truly ready for all that the world had to offer. Then there's Lucy with a statue of 5'6 160 lbs and an apple bottom that she got from her mama. She had the shoulders of a quarterback and the hands of a pianist. She was the daughter of Mr. and Mrs. Dr. Ted Fugal. Her mother was biracial mixed with Chinese and black which in turn gave Lucy her beautiful bronze skin tone free from blemish and silky hair that ran down her back. Although she was built and stack in all the right places, she would not allow her physique to be misinterpreted as a young woman whose size and shape was over compensating for lack of knowledge. This susta had a GPA of 4.06 and wasn't afraid to flaunt it with her use of elaborate words in conversation. Unknown to others Lucy embarked upon the opportunities to discuss politics with some of the most educated school staff and their affiliates just because she was bored. Then there are Naomi and Mia identical twins they were the real fun of the group they were both 5'4 125 lbs with hazel eyes and sandy brown hair. They were very petite right down to their size 5 shoes. Their ability to be comical was phenomenal. They were always telling jokes and making everyone laugh. They made jokes about everything right down to their size. They chuckled and talked about their ability to dine at any restaurant in town for the price of 12 year olds. Although their friends would all laugh when they told these jokes they knew it was their way of dealing with their very petite sizes. They were the second set of twins born to Mr. and Mrs. McNapple. Their friends always stated that they could only imagine what Mrs. McNapple must have thought after being pregnant for the second time to find out she once again carried twins. Then there was Kim standing 5'8 150 lbs golden brown skin, brown eyes and shoulder length black hair with sandy brown highlights. She had an ideal build; all her measurements ending in even numbers 36, 24, 36 she was the advisor of the group. Her parents, Mr. and Mrs. McMillan were both in the field of education which some kind of way translated to her as be the professional advisor of her group of friends. Kim honestly thought this was her purpose, to give advice to all those who would and wouldn't listen. As they all sat down on the bleachers Kim gave her friends a smile which must have indicated she had been off in her own little world. As soon as Kim smiled her friends mention to her the fact which she must have not been listening to a word which was said because the response was not that which was warranted. As Kim quickly responded with, "huh"? "Never mind" Stephanie said; as they all sat watching the game until it was over. The game ended at 10:30 pm the guys rap it up because they knew the lights on the courts shut off promptly at 10:45pm. After the game Stephanie ran over to Roger and they begin doing that annoying thing they do, rubbing heads together and kissing. Stephanie always knew how to stroke Roger's ego by telling him he was the star of the game. Everyone else knew better they knew the reality; that in fact Roger's game sucked. It was only the influence of his older brother Fredrick that prompted the guys to even let him on the courts to play with them. After the game Roger introduced the girls to his brother and his college friends who had up until this point had been just a bunch of cute guys gawking at them. There was Mike who was 6'1 build like a black version of *Batista*. Then there is Chauncey who was 6'3 who was built like *David Justice* that fine professional baseball player, Next there's Phillip who was 6'0, slim, trim in all the right places with a pack of abs so tight they look like a brand new wash board, Fredrick Roger's older brother was 6'2 mysteriously handsome with his slanted green eyes, butter cream smooth, glistening caramel colored skin and biceps the size of tree trunks and of course there was Roger. Although Roger favored his brother they did not have the same build, Roger was a bit on the puny side. The guys all stood around allowing hormones and the curiosities of the opposite sex take control over their creative young minds. Meanwhile the girls laughed about how many shots Roger missed during the game. They all talked for about 10 minutes until which the lights on the courts clicked off. Then Mike suggested they all continue their conversations at *Mildred's Soul Food* restaurant. The girls agreed and followed the guys in Phillip's tricked out 1990 Cutlass. They all arrived at Mildred's restaurant a little after 11:00pm. The girls pulled into the parking lot very slow. They could see the guys passing around a small canister of breathe spray and the girls watched as they wiped the sweat off their glistening bodies. After arriving to a neighboring parking spot the girls exited the car slow and gracefully as if they were top models being called out on stage one by one. Stephanie of course wasting no time jumped out of the car and ran over to Roger she grabbed his hand saying lets go. The girls knew why Stephanie liked being the first to sit. She would always want to sit facing the window for what she called the perfect view. Stephanie also liked to sit on the inside of the booth she always had some strange explanations for her compulsive behavior which never made sense to anyone but her. The rest of the guys and girls stood outside for 2 minutes trying to choose up their honorary dates for the night. The girls decided they would sit next to the guy that they felt was attractive enough to occupy their time for the next hour or so. Kim just wanted to sit next to the guy she felt was the least likely to hit on her. Of course she would pretend to be interested when he indulged her with the most boring conversation. Nevertheless it was one night and unless things went undoubtedly well between the guy she choose she wouldn't have to worry about seeing him again. Lucy and Phillip hit it off ever so quickly it seemed as if they had known each other for years and they had so much in common. The young inquisitive apprentices all sat around discussing hobbies, careers, life, likes and dislike as Charlotte the waitress walks over to take their orders. "May I start y'all off with something to drink?" Phillip responded with "yes

ma'am aaahh let us get a couple pitchers of beer please."
It was at that moment Kim began to realize that they
were practically on dates with older men. She had never
actually been on a date let alone with anyone older. She
looked at the others who seemed to be too busy having
a conversation to notice what had happened. Clearing
her throat she said; "excuse me they don't speak for me
and may I have a sweet tea with a slice of lemon please?"
Charlotte nodded her head in acknowledgement, "Is
there anyone else who would like something else to
drink?" The other girls followed Kim's lead "yes ma'am
sweet teas for us also," they responded and Charlotte
quickly walked away. Then Kim coughed twice and
excused herself from the table looking at the girls as
they related to the signal for them to excuse themselves.
When the girls arrived to the restroom they all begin
talking at such a rate that neither of them could
understand the other. After about 15 seconds of this
they all begin to laugh and Kim mentioned that no one
seemed to notice when Phillip ordered beer for the
entire table. Upon mentioning this they didn't seem to
care yet, Kim was very concerned. She knew that they
all had at least one parent who consumed one or more
alcoholic beverages a day. Therefore she was aware of

the unconscious statements that would come out of the mouths of those who were slightly delusional from the intoxicating drink of choice. Naomi and the others begin to laugh and talk about what they thought of the guys. Stephanie wasn't amused by their little school girl crushes and proceed to return to the booth. The rest of them stood there talking about what they would say and do if these guys consumed a little too much to drink and things got a little uncomfortable. They decided that if things were to get a little too hot to handle they would all make up some kind of excuse to leave, putting the pressure of Stephanie to take them all home therefore she would be over ruled if Roger tried talking her into staying just a little while longer. As they walked back to the table the guys were so engulfed in conversation they had barely noticed when the girls returned. To the girls surprise when their appearance became apparent to the boys they all stood up like perfect gentlemen and allowed them to sit before returning to their conversation. Charlotte the waitress walks over when the girls return to take their orders. Everyone sort of took to the person on their left as they were getting to know each other a little better. After eating they had all decided it was time to end the night. The guys had to go back to their dorms to prepare for a long day of training tomorrow. They were all on the same athletic scholarship which required them to have curfews, steer clear of agents, and not to enter into coercion through gift acceptance. "If you guys are so keen on following the rules with curfew and whatnot why on earth would you all sit up the night before a long day of training and drink alcohol; Kim asked?" "Well excuse us coach, yet we thought since we are already restricted from everything else we would at least have a drink or two so as not to be completely cut off from the world." The guys all laughed at the entertainment in which Phillip and Kim seem to provide with their back and forth chastisement. Roger trying to ease the tension mentions to Kim; "man cut them some slack these guys played ball and train like they were already entered in the NBA draft pick." "The coach is always trying to kill them and work them to death." "That's fine I just thought that anything worth having is worth working for and waiting for and beside they are not my problem," said Kim. The girls on the other hand didn't have an issue with going home late because they had all arranged to spend the night at Stephanie's parents home. They weren't worried about being scolded because her parent's went to bed with the chickens. They all expressed what a wonderful time they had and how it was different to be in the company of older sophisticated men. Some of them took the liberty of exchanging numbers and they all gave friendly and ever so innocent hugs goodnight. Upon their arrival to the car they notice that Roger was sitting inside with Stephanie each of them going at it, groping and playing tongue tag the girls cleared their throats and said, "good night Roger!" He smiled and said, "Good night haters; I mean um, ladies." As the girls headed for Stephanie's house they all talked about their experience and the differences in the guys they spent time with tonight compared to the ones they saw everyday at their high school. As they drew nearer to Stephanie's house they could see the porch light on. To their surprise as they pulled into the driveway they observed Stephanie's parents with folded arms eagerly anticipating their return. As they slowly exited the car they could hear Stephanie say under her breath "ya'll say we had a flat! Say we had a flat tire." Mrs. Strom ushered the girls into the house with Mr. Strom closely in tow. They went inside and all took a seat on the couch when Mrs. Strom said, "now I know ya'll are getting older but don't let ya'll ages start making ya'll smell your musk." This was something all the elders said when they felt as if a child was acting a little too mature before their time. Then to their surprise she stopped scolding them and sent everyone to bed, but halting Kim for a brief minute. She asked her; "Kim how you doing baby"? She could sense something was wrong because this was very unusual. Then she responded; "Is there something wrong"? Mrs. Strom then burst into tears weeping and unable to talk. Kim didn't know what was about to happen but she knew it wasn't good. Mr. Strom put his hand on her shoulder and said; "Kim, have a seat baby we've got something to tell you.

CHAPTER 2

Kim didn't remember when she hit the floor and had no knowledge that she had fallen but moments after hearing the news it seemed as if she was dreaming and that she would wake up at any moment. After asking them what happen and how did she get down on the floor she heard the words that she would remember for the rest of her life.

"Kim your father was killed today in a 10 car pile up on the interstate near Nocatee." "Your mother has gone to Nocatee County Morgue to identify the body." They continue talking and telling her everything they knew regarding the accident and the information which had been conveyed to them. Kim's body had gone completely numb. She could no longer hear anything. She knew everyone was talking because by this time she could see all her friends had rejoined her and Stephanie's parents in the living room attempting to console her. Kim didn't remember much those 12 hours before her mother return from Nocatee. Kim did however remember the devastating look her mother had on her face the day she arrived to pick her up. Her mother had huge bags under her eyes; her hair was completely a mess. She had the appearance of a woman who had been working out all day and forgot to shower. In those 12 hours her mother looked as if she had lost 20 lbs. With tear filled eyes Kim met her mother half way across the Strom's front yard with her arms out like a three year old waiting to be picked up. At that moment her mother's hug felt like the comfort of one of those warm blankets they give you out of the heater in the hospital. They must had been standing in the middle of the yard crying for about 10 minutes before Mrs. Strom came out and invited them in for some lunch. Mrs. Strom and Kim's mother begin to hug and cry. Mrs. McMillan and Mrs. Strom had been friends since middle school much like Stephanie and Kim the too of them were very close. Kim knew her father was gone and she would never hear his voice or see his smiling face again yet, the presence of her mother made her feel as if everything was alright. After they devoured their lunch Mrs. McMillan took a shower as both she and Kim prepared to head home. Although the drive from the Strom's residence to the McMillan home wasn't very far approximately 35 miles total distance it seemed to take forever to get there. As they traveled home Kim began to question her mother about her father's accident. Kim knew it was hard for her mother to deal with these questions so soon, yet the desire to know what happen overwhelmed her even more. Kim wanted to know how the accident happened and was it her father's fault. The anticipation of knowing the truth was tearing her apart she wanted to know was it his fault or the fault of some careless person with total disregard for her father's life. Mrs. McMillan explained the accident as the investigating officer told her. She said that Mr. McMillan had been caught in the middle of the 10 car pile up and from his investigation he had no knowledge of what happen to him for he was hit with such an impact of force that he had died instantly. He was traveling in the northbound lane when a car jumped the median hitting a truck carrying hazardous chemicals causing it to flip over which begin the inevitable pile up that stole her father's life. Kim then asked the devastating question "Mom do you think daddy knows he's dead?" "Kimberly Elisha McMillan shut up!" Kim knew the moment those words flew out of her mouth that they were just the words her mother needed to push her over the edge. She'd apologized a million times and ever so quickly but the damage was already done her mother begin to cry so hard her shoulders begin to shake uncontrollably as if she was going into insulin shock. Kim talked her mother into pulling over and she rapped her arms around her. The two of them sat parked on the side of the freeway trying to comfort and console one another. Mrs. McMillan explained to Kim that her father had talk to her just last week about retiring. She was trying to convince him that he was still in the prime of his life and too young to retire. Kim explained to her mother that her father being on the road at that time was not her fault and that even if she had not expressed her desire for him to continue working it didn't mean he wasn't going to continue to work anyway. No matter how they tried to rationale their thoughts of her father's death they both knew that he wasn't coming back. After they regrouped and mentally pulled themselves together her mother pulled back on to the freeway and they continue heading for home. As they pulled into the drive way she heard her mother breathe in very deep and release a huge sigh as if to say; "This house is no longer a home because her father wouldn't be there." She turned off the car and took the keys out if the ignition. Her mother just sat there and stared at the front door. "Ma come on." Her mother just sat there, Kim shook her shoulder "ma come on we got to deal with this sometime." Kim truly knew the reality was that they couldn't stay outside in the car forever. As they walk towards the door it felt as if they were both taking steps to the end of a cliff and getting ready to jump to their deaths. Kim unlocked the door and opened it wide enough for her mother to walk through and after what seemed like minutes she finally stepped through the thrush hold and smile as if to say, I did it and now everything is going to be alright. As soon as Kim brought in the last bag from the car the phone rang and seemed to continue ringing non-stop for hours afterwards with calls of condolences. Kim answered the phone only to hear the voice of her noisy cousin Tina from California calling to say she heard about the accident on the news. The reality was she had not heard it on the news yet she had heard the news from their other noisy cousin Bertha that lived about six minutes away from the McMillan's home. Bertha always seemed to be the first to find out every thing she even knew when Kim's gold fish petey died four years ago. Bertha was so noisy and a little off balanced she brought over fried fish and cornbread when petey died asking if she could give the eulogy. Nevertheless despite it all her information tended to be very accurate. Kim's mother asked her to go to the garage to retrieve the cots and extra blankets because they were sure to have relatives coming in from all over in a few days. Mrs. McMillan wanted to make sure they would all have a comfortable place to sleep when they got in town. At about 11'oclock in that morning Kim heard voices. She didn't know who was there but she knew she heard voices. Kim quickly grabbed a pair of sweat pants and a T-shirt and made her way to the bathroom. After showering and getting dressed she went to the kitchen where she noticed a bunch of faces she hadn't seen in years. There was her Aunt Sasha, Uncle Nate, and Uncle Danny her father's brothers and sister. "Hey niece, we were wondering when you was going to wake up." "When did you all get here?" Kim asked. "Early dis morning bout 4:30." "Gurl you getting tall jus like yo` daddy!" Kim's Aunt Sasha turns to her brother Danny and said, "ain't she Dank?"

Kim's father and siblings were all born in raised in the small town of Birmingham, Alabama or as they all referred to it as the "*B. ham bottom.*" Because of their southern up brining they all carried a heavy and darkly rich rooted linguistic manner of dialect. Kim's aunt walks over and kisses her on the cheek with bacon grease around her mouth.

"I can't stay small forever" Kim says, with a half smile placed on her face to cover the pain in her heart. Although she was pleased to see her aunt and uncles they only reminded her of her father's death. "Hey niece tell me something you still writing that there poetry stuff you be writing?" "Yes sir, Uncle Danny." "Good," he says; "one day you gonna make your mama rich." "You gonna to show me some of dem fo' I leave here?" "Yes sir," Uncle Danny.

"I didn't know you write poetry" her aunt Sasha said. "I don't talk about it much because it's just something I do for fun." "I'd love to hear some of it too if you don't mind." "Yes ma'am" Kim said, as she heard the door bell ringing. She walked to the door and there stood Stephanie, Roger and Fredrick they had all drove over to check on Kim and her mother. Although Kim mentioned a phone call would have been fine she was ever so pleased to see her best friend standing in the door way. She invited them in and introduced them to her uncles and aunt. Her mother invited them in for breakfast as they walked toward the kitchen. Fredrick said; "much ablidged ma'am, Kim said, "much a who?" Then she heard her uncle laughing. As he says; "boy you must have been raise round some old folks." "Yes sir," Fredrick responded. He explained that his grandparents raised them when their parents went overseas to study ancient Egyptian Artifacts 7 years ago. Kim thought to herself, it was very comforting to have people around during this very depressing time in their lives. They all talked and laughed about the good times in their lives and the way her father would always be the life of every gathering. They all made reference by way of stating, "If he was here now what he would say." After breakfast Kim and her friends begin to clear the table and wash the dishes to make it a little easier for her mother. Kim's uncles and aunt talked her mother into getting dressed and going out for the day to face one of her fears. Kim's mother had to shop for her father a suit for his burial. Kim's uncles and aunt had to assist in the difficult process as well as making the final decision for the funeral. Despite Kim's efforts to just stay at home her friends seemed to be the honorary persuasion coaches for doing the same for her getting her out of the house and getting her mind off the horrific, traumatic heartbreaking pain of the sudden death of her father. After Stephanie convinced Kim to get dressed they all sat talking to her family about their afternoon plans and discussed meeting back at the house for dinner at a feasible hour. Stephanie, Roger, and Fredrick were all very comforting. They drove over to the North Port Mall to shop for a dress for Kim to wear for her father's funeral. Of course Stephanie was the shopping guru therefore anything that Kim decided to purchase would have to have her stamp of approval at least she thought so. The girls ventured into *Dress for Success* to look for the perfect dress as the guys stood quietly and patiently waiting. It wasn't until that moment that Kim decided to ask Stephanie out of curiosity; "Why in the world is Fredrick with y'all," she replied? "He heard about your father's death when Roger was talking to me over the phone and he wanted to make sure you were O.K." Although Kim was very shocked at his compassion she was also moved. After forty minutes Kim found what she considered to be the perfect dress it was a very silky and sleek black and white spaghetti strap Versace that hugged her body and accentuated her curves with a matching jacket. Kim put on the dress and stood in the mirror. Although the dress was beautiful she thought about the reason she was buying the dress in the first place. As she stood staring at herself she reflected back to the day her father took her to the mall to buy her first prom dress for the junior high school dance and how although he didn't want her to go but he took her to buy the dress anyway just to see the smile on her face. Kim then had a black out and the next thing she knew she was sitting in a chair as one of the store clerks was handing Stephanie a cup of water as Fredrick and Roger fanned her. "Would you like for me to call the paramedic's;" said the clerk. "No thanks, she will be fine Stephanie says. "Kim, hey girl are you ok?" Kim responded by nodding her head and asking Stephanie to promise she wouldn't mention any of this to her mother. Kim didn't want her mother to worry about her. Kim then proceed to pay for her dress and bought matching shoes before deciding to call it a day and head for home. On the way Kim could hear Roger and Stephanie discussing Stephanie picking up the girls and staying the night with Kim. Meanwhile Fredrick and Roger would return home as they agreed. The four of them headed for Kim's house. When they arrived Kim's mother was still out and Stephanie said that she was going to drive the boys home. Kim gave them all hugs and a kiss as she said goodbye. "I'll come back later with the girls;" Stephanie said. Kim shook her head to acknowledge that she heard Stephanie and walked into the house. As Kim sat alone in the living room on the couch she turned on the T.V waiting for her mother, aunt and uncles to return. She realized this was the first time she had been alone in the house since her father was killed. She walked up to her mother's room door and slowly pushed the door open. She didn't know what she expected to see but apart of her wanted to see her father sitting on the edge of the bed taking off his shoes after work like he always did. She saw the picture of her father that her mother had been holding the night prior. She walked over and picked it up. She looked at the picture in stared in her father's eyes and at that moment she thought she heard a voice say in a soft whisper "I will always be right here." Oh no, she said I am not going down that road. I know you are dead in there is no way I am going to even pretend that I heard that!

She place the picture back onto the night stand close the door and went to her room and close the door there she pulled out her poetry note book and begin to review all the poems she had written. She began reading them one by one until she heard a knock at the door. "Who is it?" She didn't hear anyone respond so again she said "Who is it?" No one responded so she got up and walked over to the door. She opened the door and no one was there. So she shut the door and lie down on her bed staring at the pages in her notebook again she heard a knock. "O.K somebody has jokes if I come out swinging you'll stop playing wont you?" Then again there was no response. Picking up the phone she called Stephanie the phone rang twice and she heard; "what's up, you O.K?" Kim spoke with terror in her voice because when she said; "No." Stephanie paused and said, "O.k. I'm on my way." Kim thought to her self Stephanie must have stop at the store on her way before leaving or she had broke several laws getting to her house because in a matter of four in a half minutes she was knocking on the door. "Kim! Kim! Its Stephanie open up the door!" "SSSSSh be quiet" Kim said, "I think some one is in my house." Stephanie signal for Roger and Fredrick to come quick.

"Did you call the police?" "No, because I don't know if anyone is actually hear." "If I call the police and I don't know if anyone is in here they are going to think I am crazy." "That don't make sense Nee Nee." Kim only called Stephanie Nee Nee when she was worried because Stephanie's middle name is Denise. Kim explain to them what happen with the door and Stephanie stated that maybe it was someone outside in the neighbor's yard which made sense, although she explained it sounded as if they where knocking on her room door. Stephanie then stated that they would stay with Kim until her mother, aunt, and uncles arrived just in case she heard the noise again this way she would have witnesses. Around 5 o'clock that evening Kim's mother, aunt, and uncles arrived with loaded arms. Kim and her friends all pitched in to help bring in things from the car and put them away. Kim gave Stephanie a look out the corner of her eye as to say please don't say a word about today when her mother asked how their day went. Although Mrs. McMillan freely admitted being tired she slowly sashayed to the kitchen and prepared to cook dinner. Despite her physical and mental state of being Mrs. McMillan mustarded up the strength to entertain Kim and her friends by way of to asking them how their day went Stephanie stated, "After Kim found a dress we all just decided to hang out here."

Kim's mother was pleased to hear her friends were so supportive. Mrs. McMillan then invited Stephanie and the guys to stay for dinner. Stephanie stated, "Mrs. McMillan it's getting late and I have got to get the guys home." After further assertion of Mrs. McMillan's decisive negotiating for them to stay Stephanie agreed. "I need to call my parents to get permission." "I will call everyone's parents and get permission so there is it settled you all will stay and I don't want to hear another word about it. "After dinner everyone sat around talking and their conversations ran late into the night. Kim's mother loved all the company Kim thought it was her mother's way of having an excuse to not to deal with the loneliness she felt from not having Kim's father around. She had advised Stephanie, Roger and Fredrick to stay over because the drive during this time of night would be too dangerous. Kim's aunt and uncles prepared to leave to go back to their hotel. They all shared hugs, kisses and handshakes said goodbye and goodnight Mrs. McMillan proceeded to call the Strom's and Addison's to receive their approval for an overnight stay of Stephanie and the guys before heading off to bed. Kim pulled out the extra blankets and provided a demonstration of how to open up the let out couch and cots for the guys. She quickly walked down the hall to prepare the other side of her bed for Stephanie to sleep. Preparing the other side of the bed that meant that she had to quickly remove all the teddy bears she still slept with. About 8:30 pm her mother prepared to go to bed and warned them not to stay up too late. Mrs. McMillan gave Kim and her friends' hugs, kisses and thanked them for staying over. Kim then walked her mother down the hall to her room placed a soft kiss on the cheek as she went to her room. This was the room her mother and father had shared for the last 17 years and she knew it was going to be hard for her to go in and sleep peacefully without him. Kim hugged her tightly and said; "Mom I love you." Mrs. McMillan looked at her and smiled and said goodnight. Kim and her friends stayed up for several more hours before calling it a night.

CHAPTER 3

ABOUT 2:00am Kim heard a strange nose at first she thought Stephanie had left the bed to pull some act of romance in the middle of the night with Roger but to her surprise Stephanie was still in the bed next to her very much asleep. Kim sat up in the bed when she realized the nose she heard was that of her mother. She tiptoed into the hall and she stood next to her mother's room door she could hear her talking and crying as she peeked through the crack in the door she saw her crying and talking to a picture of her father asking him why he had to leave them. Her mother's tear stained face seemed to look more stressed than ever. The area around her mothers temples match that of her eyes they were sunken and vein filled. Kim stood there with tears in her eyes thinking about the pain her mother must be feeling as she quietly recited one of the poems she had written once when she felt as if she was alone in the world.

"Desperate paralyze screams for attention

Looking beyond a horizon of guilt free hope

A souvenir from memorable vacation leads to compassion for the wilted mind of a confused state of a sane man

Passive aggressiveness as frustrated tempers expresses themselves during a nurturing time of depression

This is a time for night to turn into day

Children rob a store just to fill their stomachs of hunger which ends in a battle to take their last breathe

A mother screams for sorrow and a wish to turn back the hands of time for this is a time for night to turn to day

A father with all hope lost and a last chance over shadowed by the color of his skin makes a decision to shorten his struggle with one blast of steel to the central nervous system that helps him to sustain this is a time for night to turn into day."

Just when she was about to push open the door to comfort her mother she felt a hand on her shoulder.

Kim turned around and there was Fredrick standing there with one finger over his lips giving her the sign to be quite. He whispered in Kim's ear; "your mother has been up for at least 3 hours crying and talking to your father's picture."

"It's best not to bother because this is her way of healing." As Fredrick pointed in the opposite direction and they quietly went to the kitchen. Kim asked Fredrick, "How do you know this?" He explained to her that this was his course of study. He said he was learning about Psychology and Human Behavior in college and upon graduation he was going to be a psychiatrist. When Kim first met Fredrick she thought he was all muscles and no brains but the more she talked with him she soon discovered that he was a pretty cool guy. As they sat talking and sometimes pausing just to share simple and quiet moments enjoying each others company Kim and Fredrick begin learning more about each other than even their closest friends knew about either of them. Kim stood up quietly with a glazy sparkle in her eye and offered Fredrick some cake and sweet refreshing orange juice to wash it down. He gladly accepted; as they sat drinking juice and nestling every morsel of delectable moist orange pound cake they decided it was time to head off to bed at which Kim suggested she was going to have a look in on her mother who by this time had fallen asleep with the picture of my father in her arms. Kim thanked Fredrick for his very intellectual conversation and headed off to bed. Kim didn't know what it was about the conversation she had with Fredrick yet, she couldn't stop thinking about him. Eventually she too dosed off only to wake up hours later with Stephanie trying to lift her eye lids asking was she going to stay in bed all day. Kim gently opens her eyes as she recites:

"It's always a pleasure to be seen as a need. You reach out for a goal and beyond a wholesome plead. Walking on a beaten foot path just to see a beautiful image of an envisioned course of action that everyone has seen. Waiting for a wonder to fill an empty mind. While whistling a song of mischief that has crossed a frozen heart with revenge that is benign. A shadowed pattern reflects a lesson which fails watching the waters of the river cast off a familiar smell." Stephanie responded with a dazed look; "What?" "Gurl get up!" By the smells coming from the kitchen Kim knew that was going to be impossible to stay in bed she could smell the scents of blueberry waffles, hot crispy bacon and scrambled eggs. "Mmmmmm mama's cooking breakfast;" She said as she rolled out of bed. "Hey! What happen between you and Fredrick last night nasty?" Stephanie always seemed to have a long life habit of asking questions that made people just want to respond ever so quickly they way she worded this seem to make even the strongest of her accompanist respond defensively. "What? Huh? Nothing happened;" said Kim. "Girl, what are you talking about?" "Mmmmmhh I bet;" "Why was he trying to look in here to see if you were awake on his way to the bathroom this morning?" "I don't know?" Kim said with a grin; "Maybe he was just trying to see if I was ok." "I bet" Stephanie said; "oh you gone tell me," she says. Kim smiled in walked away looking back over her shoulder saying, "there is nothing to tell." Although that was the truth; there wasn't anything to tell, just the fact that Stephanie thought there was provided all the excitement Kim needed. Kim winks one eye and recites another one of her poems.

"Silver line in a grey cloud, mysterious scents with sources unfound. A ground made solid to shake with the wind domination of the prayerless child whose skin I can't live in. Searching for a truth to a University of captivation spins; as the sensations of untold stories fester within.

Lost in a never ending battle that was not your own, wishing for a path that would lead to home. Doctor by the same person that is you, for the knowledge of a distant understanding an aborted clue. I run as fast as the wind even speeder than light; as you run away in a time that deserved an untailored fight. I walk backwards through the scenes that emulated you as you run away in time just to make through."

"Wow!" Stephanie responds; "You are truly nuts." As she leaves the room quickly lowering her head to miss the pillow which is now airborne from Kim's bed. At about 9 o'clock Kim's aunt and uncles showed up refreshed for another day of travels to handle funeral arrangements for her father. This time they were all going to head over to the funeral home. Kim volunteered to go with them but, her mother insisted that I spend time with my friends and relax until the viewing. She followed her mother's directions because it never crossed her mind that she would have to go and view the body until that very moment in which the words were spoken. She said O.k. with a half smile praying not to break down in tears in front of her friends. She sat down at the table next to Stephanie and across from Fredrick. Stephanie looked at Kim as she said good morning to Roger and Fredrick. She then grins as if to be saying, "I know something is going on." Kim looked at Stephanie then at Fredrick and smiled as he tipped his glass at her. "Mmmmmhh" Stephanie's grumbles under her breathe. The breakfast was in credible; Kim thought. She ate her mother's cooking all the time although this particular morning it just seemed to take her taste buds to new heights. The waffles were moist and so full of soft plum blueberries. The eggs were soft, tender and golden; the bacon was crisp and flavorful the food seemed to explode in to a medley of delicious flavors as she chewed very slow enjoying ever morsel. Kim and her friends made plans to hang out for a few hours before they were due to head back across town.

They cleaned up the house, rolled away the fold up bed, the boys freshened up as Stephanie showered and change into some of Kim's clothes. Stephanie and Roger made up some kind of excuse to disappear as Fredrick and Kim cleaned up the kitchen.

Kim washed and Fredrick rinsed. They talked about everything from life, death, dreams and wishes. Kim couldn't believe that in the little time they had spent together she had shared things with him that it had taken months for her to share with her closest friends. For some strange reason she felt really close to him. He was a real gentlemen he never tried to hit on or touch her in a sexual way. In fact he just really seemed to enjoy her company and she enjoyed his. Fredrick was very attractive and if Kim was going to choose a person to spend her time with she would want it to be some one like him. They talked and talked and they were really connecting. They discovered they had a lot of the same interests and cared about some of the same things such as world peace, change, art, poetry and romance novels. When it was time for her friends to leave Kim looked around for Stephanie and Roger.

Of course they were in the bathroom with the door locked. She knocked on the door *boom! boom! boom! boom! boom! boom! boom!* "Stephanie Olivia Denise Strom you and Roger better not be in there disrespecting my mother's house!" "Of course we aren't Roger was still hunger so I was giving him a snack before we hit the road." She burst out laughing as she open the door revealing that she was merely helping him bust pimples on his face. They all laughed and headed towards the front door. "Oh wait! I need to leave my mom a note to let her know where I am going just in case she comes back before I do." "O.k. we will meet you in the car;" Stephanie says as they all head for the door. When they arrived in St. James City Stephanie dropped the guys off. Stephanie and Kim drove to her house where she called the other girls over to meet them. Naomi, Lucy and Mia all made it over to Stephanie's house about 2:30pm to complete the mob squad. They hung out for a few hours talking about life and how precious it is and how they wouldn't know what to do if they were in Kim's shoes. Kim didn't mind expressing herself for some reason she felt that it was now her time to break down and face her father's death head on and who better then her girls to be there to support her.

The day of the viewing Stephanie, Lucy, Mia, Naomi, Kim's aunt and uncles drove over together to give Kim and her mother some time to deal with our emotions. Kim and Mrs. McMillan talked, laughed and cried as they rode over to the funeral home. They reflected on the kind of man her father had been. Upon their arrival to the funeral parlor there were many of Mr. McMillan's friends from work and family members from all over and who else to be the first one at the door waiting to get in but ol' nosiy cousin Bertha. Look! Mrs. McMillan stated; pointing toward the entrance of the funeral parlor door. "Boy, I tell you this woman don't miss a beat." Kim walked to her mother's side of the car and grabbed her hand "come on mom we gotta deal with this." As tears streamed down her mother's face Kim could feel her pain and as much as she tried to be strong for her mother she felt her own emotions getting the best of her and she too began to cry as they walked towards the door. It felt as someone had poured cement around her feet and it was beginning to harden with ever step. At one point she felt her mother tugging on her as if to say keep moving. The funeral home director explain to the two of them upon arrival that if they didn't want to do it at this time they could wait and view the body after everyone was gone but her mother insisted that they were going to do it and they were going to do it now. Kim didn't know why but as she looked at the funeral director the thought flashed across her mind about how the people that work in funeral homes always look like they were dead. She had to refocus and regain her composer because her mother needed her as they slowly approached the casket Kim could see the terror on her mother's face as she halted. Her Uncles quickly stepped up and grabbed her mother's hand as Kim's aunt Sasha took her hand and embraced her and walked slowly behind her mother. As Kim and her mother finally reached the casket she looked down at her father and begins to weep like a newborn baby as Mrs. McMillan turned to her brother-in-law Nate and questioned why? Nate embraced Mrs. McMillan with the infamous *God knows best* phrase. Then it was finally Kim's turn to see her father as she and her aunt walked up to the casket; initially Kim thought it was all just a dream, and then she imagined her father just lying there asleep. Finally she reached in to touch his hand and they were so cold. His face expressed a very peaceful emotion. She reached in and touched his face it was stiff and cold and his cheeks looked as if they had been stuffed with cotton. As the tears rolled down her face her aunt tried pulling her away and her feet wouldn't move. She wanted to walk away but her feet would not allow her body to move. All of a sudden Kim's mouth opened and words were coming from them but Kim couldn't hear herself as she spoke the words:

"I step into life a big world with fins ready to shred my emotions again and again. Look into the time of past and a future you may see. A glimmering light with no dignity and hope for a soul like me finding a gift to keep and a secret to hide in the matter when I close my eyes. I focus on mysteries and stories of untold truth. In a big world with a small view and feeling fixated on you. A path carved out for a mountain of emotions wishing for a forecast of unforgivable notions. The robe of a goal gets smashed by a rolling prediction, of what your life could be with or without you for dependency. Wait to take a walk with your best friend and you will soon see a life of feeling small in a big world for me."

She never heard her own words and in her mind nothing was clear she blacked out for a moment only to come to and hear words amplified three times over. She began telling her father that she was there and that he needed to get up "Wake up daddy! Wake up daddy! We miss you! Daddy please don't leave us, we need you!" She didn't know when or how she was pulled away but shortly there after she could remember being rocked in her mother's arms like a newborn baby crying. She heard Stephanie, Naomi, Lucy and Mia ask if it was o.k. for them to come in the director approached her uncle Danny and asked if it was ok to let them in and he nodded in response to say yes as they ran to her rescue. The wake was full of all of her father's friend's family and co-workers whom had all come to show their respects and to offer words of consolidation regarding whatever they thought about Kim's father. It was also the first stage in the healing process for Kim and her mother. The night before her father's funeral was long and she couldn't sleep. Kim's aunt Sasha was staying the night to provide comfort to Kim and her mother instead of at the hotel. Her aunt slipped her mother sleeping pills as headache medicine around 8:15pm to assure she would sleep through the night. Kim pulled out her notebook and began to read a few poems to her mother as she dosed to sleep.

"My heart needs a man that will stand up and be proud of me a man to hold my hand during my most impeccable time of need. My heart needs a welcome mat where the road and the sun meet. It longs for the comfort from a lonely drive home with some one to keep me warm. My heart needs an ear on days when I just want to talk a partner to share my path on a day when I need to take a walk. My heart needs air to allow my lungs to breathe when the intoxication of hatred and pain has all but consumed me. My heart needs a hand to touch in those spots that others can't reach surpass the hurt of physical pain way down deep beneath. My heart needs a piano on day when I want to sing my heart needs a higher power much higher then the eye can see. My heart needs the Lord on the days I no longer what to be. My heart needs clear thoughts to build up strength in my knees when standing becomes too hard for me to sustain the inevitable that was meant for me. My heart needs glory on days when my mind just wants to be. More then all the rubies, diamonds, and gold the Lord is what my heart truly needs."

"Figuring out a time and place running from your mind with one wishing stone to live alone waiting for the day of strong hold flipping on your own accord just to be at home

dominance of a man just because of the organs of different grains forceful afflictions just to carry his name time that wont turn back all that is blue all because his strong hold is upon you."

"I see your face all the time but everyday is new.

Seventeen years together passed but everyday is new.

Disagreements forgotten, grey skies turned blue.

Forgetting hurtful moments because everyday is new;

I hunger and thirst for a quiet moment with you just because time is sweet and everyday is new. Joined together under the Lord's mercy a union of two just because he knew for us everyday that would pass would be new. If I didn't know your heart, couldn't read your mind or find solidarity in you I would cease to love, to live and breathe because everyday is new. Long walks in the park, sweet smells of dew I love the life I live as I spend faithful time with you. You're vigorous and fantastic and my heart still pines for you all because of the state of being makes everyday new."

After the third poem Kim glanced down at her mother who was completely asleep and she decided that now was the perfect time for her to exit. She gently kissed her mother on the forehead. She eased out of the bed and crept down the hall ever so quite not to wake her mother and aunt. She picked up the cordless phone and slipped outside so no one would hear her talking. She pressed in all the numbers and prayed that Fredrick would be the one to answer the phone. "Hello, she said in a soft whisper is Fredrick home" "This is he," the voice on the other end responded *Bingo*! She got lucky.

It was Fredrick. "Hello, did I wake you?" Clearing his throat, "No what's wrong?" "I couldn't sleep and I really needed some one to talk to." "Oh, O.K.!" He was fully awake now. "Talk to me I'm listening he said using his best psychiatrist voice." "I'm just thinking about tomorrow; you know it will be the last time I will see my father's face." "I don't think I can deal with this; it's hard you know?"

"I feel like I need to be strong for my mother but what if I can't even be strong enough for myself?" "This is a really hard time for you and your family, don't beat yourself up." "You have so many people around you who love you and your mother and no matter how you feel they are going to be there to help you through it." "Yeah, your right;" she says. "I won't hold you up; thanks for listening." "You're welcome, anytime." "Good night."

"Good night beautiful." "What," but the line went dead. "Did he just call me?" "*Dang,*" she thought. Kim wished she could call him back and ask him what he said. "Awe!" "Oh well forget it," she thought. She knew in order to face the day which lie ahead she needed to get some sleep. The day that seem would never arrived had finally approached as Kim and her mother prepared to be taken to the church by the limo her aunt and uncles made all the last minute arrangements for the rest of the family that had flown in, drove up, and rode down for this devastating occasion. As they proceed to the family car Kim felt someone touch her hand. As she turned to look around she saw Fredrick mouthing the words; "I'm here for you." She gave him a smile as a means to say thank you and got in the car with her mother. On the way to the funeral the family discussed the kind of man they all knew Mr. McMillan to be and how he would have been extremely please with the turn out. When they arrived at the church there were people standing around outside with tissues in hand crying and consoling one another. Kim clenched her mother's hand as the car rolled to a stop and glared at her with tear filled eyes and asked, "mama are you ready?" Mrs. McMillan took two deep breathes and responded; "yes baby, I'm as ready as I'll ever be." With the assistance of her two brother-in-laws Mrs. McMillan exited the car and Kim with her aunt closely in tow. As they walked towards the entrance of the church the sounds of *I'll Fly Away* became very over powering stirring up all the emotions that both Kim and her mother were trying to keep concealed. Walking down the isle seemed to become more difficult with every step. At one point Kim thought she witnessed her mother actually being dragged down the isle by her uncles like a patient in the psychiatric ward and her uncles where orderlies dragging her to her room. As her mother finally made her way around to the casket and broke down completely Kim's nerves totally became unraveled. She begins to shake and breathe heavily as she watches her mother tell her father that she loved him and gently kiss him on the lips. Kim slowly walked up to the casket and at that moment she felt a strong hand on the small of her back whispering in her ear, "tell him, let it out, it's ok beautiful he is still with you in spirit." That was the motivation she needed she bent down kissed her father's cold harden lips and told him she loved him and he would be forever missed. As Kim turned to look at the face of the hands that were holding her she fell into the open arms of Fredrick. His embrace was warm like a blanket on a cold day, it was soft like a cashmere sweater, and he smelled of *The Baron* and just for a brief second that moment he made Kim feel as if all was well. After the funeral days seem to run together and the weeks seemed to be shorter than a New York minute. After about four months her mother decided to take on another job to keep busy and to keep her mind off the passing of her husband. Kim knew her mother didn't need the money because her father had a well paid pension package. He had the retirement years invested in his job and out of respect for his memory the Ashford County School Board awarded her mother full benefits. That along with the pending lawsuit her mother had against the insurance company that insure the driver that caused her father's untimely death. They were doing fairly well so there was no other reason that Kim could see for her mom to take on an additional source of income. Kim began her final year in High school and things seem to get harder as the months progressed. Kim barely attended any of her classes. She thought some of her teachers were actually passing her out of respect for her father although he didn't teach in their county everyone knew him and loved him dearly so of course his death affected not just the county in which he had taught but in the county in which they lived as well. During her senior year Kim became very detached and she rarely saw her friends or even her own mother. When she came home from school she would go to her room and shut the door barely coming out to eat and only coming out faithfully on a routine basis to shower. Throughout it all her orderly existence and tenaciousness not to quit attending school allowed her to graduate. On the day on her graduation Kim was waiting in line for the coordinator to tell her where to stand when she got the strangest feeling like she was being watched. She turned and looked behind her and there amongst a crowd of excited graduating teenagers was Fredrick Addison. He was wearing a black jacket with patches on the elbows, a royal blue turtle neck shirt, denim Dickie blue jeans which were cuffed at the bottom and a pair of black old school suede shoes. He looked very much the part of a psychiatrist. He walked up to her and slowly leaned in to embrace her. "Congratulations," he said as she nestled in his embrace taking in a deep sniff of his cologne. If there was one thing to which she could count on it was the way Fredrick smelled. He always smelled like he had just traveled to Paris. "So how have you been?" "I've been living one day at a time;" Kim responded. "What are you planning to do with yourself after this very liberating experience called graduation?" "I'm not sure I know college is definitely in my future yet which one I'm not sure I have a bunch of acceptance letters at home I have to sift through." Fredrick stands back and laughs; "Naw mama calm down I'm talking about tonight." "Oh I don't really have any plans, my mother and I are suppose to go to dinner afterwards but that's about it" "That's cool;" he responds. "Hey listen, if you're not doing anything afterwards how about you stop by the Town Center Hall?"

"My parents have rented the place in honor of my brother graduating and they are throwing him a party." "It's going to be fun and beside your entire clan of girlfriend's is coming." "I don't know;" Kim response. "Maybe I will, Kim said; if I am up to it." "O.k. no pressure I hope you will consider it I would really like to see you there," he said.

Later that night Kim decided to stop by the Town Center to socialize with her friends for she knew that this might be their last big hoopla before they go off to college. Kim arrived around 10:30pm. "May I take your coat?" She turns around to look and it was a young man standing behind her with a ticket in hand offering to check her coat. "Yes thank you;" she responded. As she took off her coat and the light glistened off her dress for brief second it seemed as if all the eyes in the room were on her. She was wearing a white and gold satin Dolce and Gabbanna dress which hung low around her shoulders with a wide v cut down the back which ran all the way to the small of her back. She looked radiant; she carefully scanned the room for familiar faces or at least someone she could converse with to help loosen her feeling of claustrophobia. Then from across the room she catches a glimpse of none other then her friends clustered together at the punch bowl scoping the room like hens in a coop. "Honestly ladies I thought you would all have found another approach to finding prospects." The girls truly overjoyed at this point by her presence enough so to ignore her comment as the all embrace in a group hug. "Dang Kim we were hoping you would come girl we really do miss you and we didn't want to go off to college without getting together again for one last *Pow Wow!*" "Well never fear Kim is here;" she stated as they all laughed. "O.k girls lets just enjoy this night and make the most of freedom as maturing adults before reality begins to kick in;" says Mia. "I agree," says Lucy as they all proceed to the dance floor. As the night proceeds the D.J announces that he is taking final request and before the next song began to play the D.J announces: *"This is a special request by Fredrick going out to Kim get close ya'll it's time to slow whine."* The girls all turn in look to Kim as she turns around and notices Fredrick standing behind her with his hand out. "Ms. McMillan, do you mind if I have this dance?"

They all begin to clap as she gladly accepts. He slowly leads her to the middle of the dance floor pulling her body close as she leans in and says softly; "I don't know how to slow drag." "It's O.k. he says I gotchu." Their bodies were so close you could barely see where one began and the other end as they dance closely and slowly to Musiq's song: *Love Don't Change.* "I don't know what this all means right now but this feels so good;" she softly whispers in Fredrick's ear. "It's all good just go with it;" he responds. "I just feel so comfortable with you." He then grabs her face and gently kissed her innocently on the lips. His lips were so soft and warm Kim couldn't resist she leaned in and invited him to kiss her again this time she was willing to exchange his passion. She opened her mouth allowing him to taste and savor the flavor of her minty breathe as she inhaled the sweet smell of his breath which smelled like peaches. Before they knew it they were wrapped in each others arms going at each other like a married couple in a romantic movie. All of a sudden Kim felt a tap on her should and there behind her stood Stephanie and the rest of her friends with glaring eyes and opened mouths. "Ya'll need to get a room." Too embarrassed to respond they looked around the room to peering eyes and hand claps of congratulations. "I'm sorry he said I didn't mean to get carried away." "I would never disrespect you like that;" he said. "It's not your fault you didn't do anymore than I wanted you to." "I think it's time for me to leave anyways," she says. "Do you need a ride?" "Sure." Kim then walks over to her friends and says, "I think I am going to call it a night I will see you all later." "Goodnight," they all chanted. "Don't do anything I wouldn't do," Stephanie adds. "They haven't invented what you wouldn't do," Kim states jokingly. On the way to Kim's house Fredrick and Kim discuss college and her plans for the future. "Would you like to get something to eat?" "Naw I'm not really hungry." "Would you like to go for a drive?" "I'm sorry, I just don't want this night to end," he says. "Sure we can go for a drive." They pull up to Mallman Point overlooking the Westside projects. "Kim I really do like you and I have felt this way ever since the first time we met." "I don't know what it is about you." "At first I thought it was pity because of the death of your father." "I realized later that it wasn't that." "I mean the way I feel when I am around you is so hard to explain and when I am not with you I think about you all the time." He grazes the side of her face softly and gently he draws her chin to turn her head to face him as he continues; "I know I am four years older then you but I really do care for you." Kim looks at him in his eyes and she leans in and they share a hot and heavy moment. He draws her body near as he begins to rise. "You don't have to do this," he says. "I know, if it gets to be too much I will let you know," she says. He begins to slowly caress her body and press his full statute manhood on to her leg. She reaches down and caresses him feeling his length and girth she begin to feel a little unsettled. "Wait," she says. "What have you changed your mind?" "No. I... I have never, I mean I am a..." "What baby you can tell me anything, he said." She looks at him with tear filled eyes I'm a virgin and I don't know what to do once we... you know." "It's O.k I'll talk you through it." "He then opens his wallet and pulls out a condom. "Fredrick did you plan on doing this with me tonight?" "What?" "No!" "If you are having second thoughts baby we don't have to do this; I have all the time in the world to wait for you." "No, I'm O.k. I'm just a little scared," she says. "Don't be I will be very gentle." He leans her seat back all the way to an almost flat position then he slowly lowers himself on top of her. Breathing very heavily he begins to slowly insert as she flinches from the pain. "Ssssss, oh wait! wait! wait it's hurting." "O.k.," he responds. "Listen take a deep breathe and relax." Kim tried to relax but every time he inserted the pain is entirely too much to bear upon the finally try he broke through as she screamed and begin to peel the skin off his forearm. He kissed her softly on the fore head and wiped her tears as he moans. She began to shake underneath the pressure and then she pushed forcefully asking him to stop. Almost at his peak he seemed dismayed yet at her request he complied as he released a long drawn sigh of anguish. "Did we just," she asked? "Ahh physically yes, technically no, he responded." "Are you upset with me," she asked? "No baby," he responds. "Come on let me take you home." As they drove to Kim's house there was complete silence. Kim sat thinking about what and just happen as Fredrick sat thinking about what didn't happen. Upon arrival to Kim's house she thanked him for a very interesting night and he promised to call her when he arrived home. Kim walked in the house and quietly crept past the couch which her mother was laying fast asleep. She didn't want to wake her and have her ask how her night went because she was almost certain that she would have to lie. She grabbed her pajamas and quickly went into the bathroom. She discovered that her beautiful and very expensive Dolce and Gabbanna dress was ruined. There was blood all over it. As she explored her body she questioned: "Did I just get my period?" As she showered she wipe constantly to see more evidence to support her theory but there wasn't any. "What has happened to me;" she thought? After showering Kim climb into bed and waited for Fredrick to call and it never happened finally she drifted off to sleep. The next day Kim awoke to her phone ringing off the hook she look down at her alarm clock it was only 8:30am. She wondered who could be calling this early then she thought; "it must be Fredrick." She dived across the bed and answered only to hear Stephanie's voice on the other end inquiring about her happenings from the night before. "So gurl did chu give um some?" "Good morning to you too Stephanie." "Why are you calling me at... glancing the clock, 8:33am?" "So did cha, did cha, did cha, did cha?" "Would you hush; you sound like a broken record." "And you my dear are being evasive." "I know you gave him some on his last night before he gets shipped off." "Huh what are you talking about shipped off?" "Fredrick has been in boot camp for six months and he is being shipped off today at 4:00pm for a 12 month stretch in the Marines; I thought he told you?" "No he didn't;" Kim replied. As time went on the girls all chose universities of their choice and everyone went off to college. Years past and Kim and her friends seemed to lose touch as they matured and chose courses of study. After two years of community college Lucy, Mia, Naomi and Stephanie all wound up at the same University.

CHAPTER 4

*S*EVEN *years later…* Kim returns home from college. "Kimberly McMillan is that you?" She heard a voice from behind her as she sat waiting on her mom at the bus station. Kim slowly turned around to see Roger standing there. She hadn't been home that much in seven years and she could barely recognize his face he had certainly matured and grown from puny to a nice dark rippled piece of chocolate. It had been seven years since she had seen any of her high school friends and she didn't know if they would all look the same for from the looks of Roger he sure didn't. Through hazy glances and desperate reels of confusion wow those honey brown eyes and the snow white smile; it truly was Fredrick's younger brother Roger, the heart throb of Stephanie's life. "Hey Kim I haven't heard from you in a while I asked Stephanie about you and she said you hadn't been home since three months after graduation so they hadn't seen you in a while." How are you?"

"I'm ok, just needed some time and space to think about things," she explained. "Oh I understand completely, can I give you a ride somewhere?" "Naw, maybe some other time, I'm waiting on my mother." "It's ok I can drop you off at her job come on I don't mind." "I am on my way to pick up Fredrick from the airport anyways so it wouldn't be out of my way." "I don't mind honestly." Kim's skin crawled at the sound of Fredrick's name she felt so betrayed and disgusted by the thought of how he left without a noted or so much as a phone call after she gave him the very fruit of her being. "So how has he been," she asked? "Who Fredrick, Oh he is doing well." "He finished his degree in Psychology in the Marines and saved all the money he earned to come home and open up his own private practice with none other then his baby brother." "Wow that's great," she responded trying not to reveal the hurt in her voice as she spoke. "Come on let me give you a ride it's the least I could do for you since you haven't been home in what seems like forever." Kim agreed and they drove up town towards the Community Service Tower or CST building where her mother worked doing clerical work.

"So is this your car?" "Yup." "This is a nice car, BMW wow you are truly coming up in the world." "So where did you get it?" "I am in the process of buying it from Campbell's Auto Mall." "I put two thousand down on it three weeks ago sort of an early pre-private practice gift." "So what you been up to lately?" "Nothing much, looking for a place to put my law degree to work." "Yeah so is everyone else; all your girls attended the same college and are now searching for jobs." "Where did you go?" "Berkley Academy of the Arts 7 year double major program," Kim stated. "Wow, Kim you go girl!" "Hey listen, we have planned a big party tonight celebrating Fredrick returning home from the Marine Corp I hope you will come?" "I don't know; I haven't seen any of the old clan in years." As she thought to herself: "and Fredrick is the last person I want to see right now." "That's all the more reason to come tonight if you ask me?" "Here is the address hope to see you there." Kim's return home was truly a surprise welcome to her mother. Mrs. McMillan looked as if she hadn't aged a bit she looked radiant glowing smile and strong tall stance she was the same strong black woman

Kim remembered her being when she first left for college. She and her mother went out for lunch and they were playing catch up when she announced to Kim that she had some news to share with her. "Kim baby, I … I kind of met someone." "What!" "What do you mean you met someone?" "I mean that I have met someone; his name is Kenny and we have been seeing each other for about eight months now." "So… I don't know what to say this is all a surprise." "I don't know what to say ma." "I would like for you to meet him." "Ok" she stated hesitantly. "When is this endeavor to meet Mr. Kenny scheduled?" "What about tonight?" "Oh I don't know about tonight ma I just made plans to reconnect with the girls." "It's only for a few minutes Kimmy we are not going to hold you up from hanging with your friends." "Alright ma I meet Mr. Kenny." "Come on don't be like that." "Like what ma you bust the news that you seeing some guy and I am suppose to be in stitches over him or something?" "I did agree to meet the man." "Alright baby just know that he will never replace your father he just help to sooth the pain." It was great to be out again hanging with the girls, Kim thought but she still felt like something was missing things were very different for her now the good times were just memories in her mind and although the girls were trying hard to rekindle the excitement flame of friendship in their lives which had once been, Kim still seem to be distant. *"Group hug!"* the girls yelled as they all ran over to Kim as she entered the party. "I am so glad you decided to come tonight Kim, Girl we really missed you;" said Stephanie. "Yeah, I just thought I would come out for a little while." "Guurl, it's a lot of cute guys in here;" said Mia. "Yeah, I guess so." "Come on, get up on your feet and dance!" "Naw, not right now Mia, maybe later." "What's wrong with you?" "Nothing I just found out my mother is seeing some man named Kenny." "Oh Mr. Kenny I know him he is really nice Kim you need to give him a chance." "I don't know bout all that." "Ok then what about dancing?" "Naw I'm good." "Ok but you are going to get up before the night is over." "Yeah alright." As the night went on Kim begin thinking of a good excuse to exit the party when she looked across the room and noticed a guy with a very familiar face standing there watching her. As he began to get closer she started searching her mind for a reason to walk away although she thought that if see ever saw his face again she would kill him she knew that in her heart she still had feeling for him. He was her first and she wanted to know why he left her without a word. "Should I ignore him, she thought?"

"Should I walk away?" As he approached she could see his glowing white smile and very seductive lips and her body trembled. "Hey beautiful, how are you?" "Huh?"

"Are you talking to me;" Kim says as look behind her. "Yes of course;" he responded as he gently grabbed her hand to kiss it. "If it isn't the beautiful Ms. Kimberly McMilllan?" "Heeeeey...Freddy what's up?" Trying to play off the fact that she had been feeling betrayed by him. "Fredrick the name is Fredrick." "I know I was just playing." "Ha ha ha" "So how long has it been?" "Seven years, three months, twelve days and eight hours," she responded. "O.k., so how have you been?" "It is what it is; you know, just taking it one day at a time," she response. "I don't mean to be rude but do you have a date and if not would you like to dance?" "Naw I'll pass, or do you not remember what happened the last night you and I danced together?" "Come on this is my favorite song; I would love to dance with you while listening to it and besides it wasn't even like that." Melting into his glowing bright smile she could no longer refuse. As Fredrick coached her onto the floor with his one hand high in the air he yelled, "yeah;" the D.J must have read my mind." "Do you believe in omens?" "Mmmmmmmmhuh," she responded. "I believe this song was meant to play at this very moment." "What do you think?" Kim gave him a flirtatious smile as she and Fredrick danced to Jamie Foxx's *Unpredictable.* As his strong hands grabbed the small of her back she melted in his arms. The two danced close and slow as Fredrick sang in her ear with warm sweet breathe that smelled like juicy ripe strawberries. Kim melted in his arms and closed her eyes tight as she tighten her embrace and smelled the nape of his neck which was lace with the sweet smell of 99 Roca Wear cologne. After the dance they talked, laughed, and took in a mental stroll down memory lane. "You hurt me ya know?" "I waited all night for you to call me." "I felt so stupid." "I'm sorry baby, it wasn't like that I didn't want to hurt you by telling you I had to leave after we…. Ah you know." "When I called back looking for you it was too late and you had already left for college." "I never told anyone what happened between us because I didn't want anyone in our business." "Oh so we have business now," she says. "I thought you would be married with kids by now." "No, you were all I could think about." "Yeah right for seven years, get real!" "Listen I'm not looking to be hurt again, I think it's time I call it a night." "Wait!"

"Kim can I at least have your number?" "Why because you want me to sit up all night waiting for you to call like when I was a young teenager in love?" "What, naw come here let me talk to you…please?" She walked away and promptly exited the party.

"I know all that you are and all that you could be.

But do you know how much you have been to me? You are the sister that can't say no even when you can't provide. You are the sister that would keep all my secrets tucked deep inside. You are the sister who's always here unconditionally with lesson of life. Your heart is so full of compassion. You would sacrifice three fourths of your life to be with God but you would save one fourth just to safeguard my heart. You would drive up a mountain without a means to know how. On a hot day you'd wipe the sweat from a stranger's brow. You would give a smile to a day of pain.

You would welcome a hurtful moment to yourself just to spare others from feeling the pain and shame. You would work for hours without any pay. You would call eight times a day to make sure everything is ok. You would run a marathon with two broke legs if you thought that it would make my day. Regardless of all these things that you would do to please; I appreciate more then it all you being a Hero to me."

"Hello," Kim answered. "Hey gurl you still up?" Dang, she thought; "yeah I'm awake what's up?" "Oh nothing I just wanted to know if you wanted to go with us tomorrow to the step show on 750 Belmont?" "I don't know I might, I will holla at you in the morning." "Ok good night." Again the phone rings Kim dives across the bed to answer.

"Hello?" "Hey beautiful what's up?" "Nothing, wassup with you and how did you get my number?" "Please who are you kidding your mother's number hasn't changed in over the past seven years and besides the number is listed." "I am surprise you are still awake." "Yeah I am normally up until about ten o'clock." "So can I take you out for lunch tomorrow about one o' clock?" "Um I am supposed to meet up with the girls tomorrow for the step show on 750 Belmont." "Ok what about dinner?" "Why? Look I don't have time for your games?" "No but I feel like I owe you an explanation can you at least give me that." "Please that was over seven years ago and besides I was young and I'm not holding a grudge." "Nevertheless let me get this off my chest I need to apologize and tell you why." "Sure that sounds good." "What time would you like to meet?" "I can pick you up about eight?" "Make it eight thirty and you got a date." "Ok good night sweetie." "Good night." Yes yes yes! She shouted as she hung up the phone Kim was really excited about being able to possibly rekindle the flame and the chemistry that she once felt for Fredrick. Kim loved the way Fredrick made her feel when she was with him. She had to tell someone about how she felt and who better then Stephanie. "Hey Stephanie!" "What's up I thought you went to bed?" "No I'm still up." "Listen, what do you think about Fredrick?" "Cedrick who, Oh wait a minute did you say Fredrick?" "Roger's Brother Fredrick?" "Yes, I like him." "He seems to be pretty cool." "Why, you planning on hooking up with him?" "Maybe,ugh! I don't know. I got to think I will call you later." Fredrick was a very nice and gentle person who Kim definitely saw herself being able to fall for him. After the show Fredrick decided to meet up with Kim and her friends at the step show and take her out to dinner from there. They talked and he explained all that he had been through during his service in the Marine Corp. He explained to her that even though he had left she was always a constant thought in his mind. They seem to pick up there relationship right where they left off and Kim became very content with what there relationship was beginning to become.

CHAPTER 5

I T was a very hot morning so hot Kim could feel the covers sticking to her body as she rolled out of the bed thanking God she had made it to see another day. Just then the phone rang in of course who else but none other than Fredrick was on the line."Hey beautiful what's up whatcha doing today?" "I don't know yet I haven't made any plans." "What are you up to?" "Nothing much, how about you and I go get some lunch say about 1:30ish?" "I have some one I would really like for you to meet." "Wow! O.k. does he want me to meet his mother she thought to herself?" "Am I ready for this?" She questioned nevertheless she agreed. "Great, he said." "I will pick up around 11:00." "Whoa why so early?" "Well I have a surprise for you and it is going to take us a while to get there". "O.k well give me about 45 minutes I just got out of the bed." "Ok no problem see you soon, take care beautiful." "Bye Fredrick." Her heart begin to pound so hard it seem as if it would come out of her chest "I have to wear the perfect outfit don't want to seem to trashy nor do I want to seem as if I have no flavor when I meet his mother because first impressions are very important," Kim thought.

Kim turned on the radio as she began to look for her perfect outfit to meet Fredrick's mother. About an hour later Fredrick rings the door bell. Kim opens the front door dressed in a sleek and sultriest Vera Wang satin v-neck black dress accented with gold accessories. "Wow!" Fredrick states, as he looks at her from head to toe.

"You look beautiful!" "Thank you," Kim replied as she steps back through the thrush hold of the doorway with a smiling invitation for Fredrick to come in. "I just have to grab my shawl and I will be ready." As she walked away Fredrick took note of ever inch of her body from her long silky smooth legs, up to her round plump apple bottom, small sleek waist, and perky sized 38C's. Kim slowly walked to the room down the hall almost certain that Fredrick was watching as she walked away slightly glimpsing behind to catch him staring as she walked away she grabbed her shawl from the bed gently and slowly lacing her neck, breast, and mid section with her favorite perfume *"Usher"* for women. She slowly walked down the hall coaching her self through the very tense moment she felt was ever before her on this trip to his mother's house. "Ok I'm ready." "Alright let's go," said Fredrick as he stood to his feet to open the door. As she moved he watched her every detail. He opened her car door and quickly strides to the driver side and they were off. "Are you nervous?" "Don't be my mother is very sweet and she has been waiting to meet you." "Do I look Ok?" Kim stated, as she fixed her shawl to be sure not to reveal too much skin. "No!" "You look better then O.k. you look beautiful." Kim gave him a big smile as she stepped out of the car. A little boy darted from behind the fence yelling, "their here!" "Aunt PegSue their here!" "That's just my little cousin Damien," Fredrick stated. "How many people are here?" Kim began to question as the noise from the house picked up the closer they got to the door. "Oh, just 35 people or so we are having sort of a family gathering," he said. "That's my surprise I wanted you to meet my whole family." "I talk about

you so much they have all been waiting to meet you."
"Wait, what do you mean we have only been seeing each
other for a few months how could they know so much
about me already?"

"Maybe that is the way you see it but the night we all
met on the courts was the first time you and I started
seeing each other." "Sure there have been several
years since then but you are all that I have spoken of
since that time and my family was beginning to think
you were a myth." "Roger knew I was in love with a
girl yet I never revealed your name because he would
have told Stephanie and of course she would have told
the entire world." "I didn't tell you how I felt before
because I always knew I wanted to go into the Marine
Corp and I didn't want to start a relationship with you
before leaving because that wouldn't have been fair to
you or me." This way there would be know pressure
on you to feel obligated to wait for me when I went to
the Marine Corps. The way I figured it, if it was meant
to be, you would be single when I got home and true
as the day is blue you were." "So you trying to tell me
you had this whole thing planned since the day you saw
me at the party?" "No it's nothing like that what I'm
saying is you were the one I had in my heart." "So what

are you saying?" Truth be told I love you I have always loved you since the first day I met you. I just never said anything because not many people believe in love at first sight. To be honest I didn't even know what I was feeling." "Wow that is a lot to take in," she says. "I know and I'm sorry to have to break it down to you like this but I didn't want you to think this was something I do often bring chicks home to meet my mother. You don't have to do this if you don't want I am more then willing to excuse myself and take you where ever you want to go." "No, I am fine I just never knew how you felt and hearing it all now it's just overwhelming." "I always had thoughts of you and I knew that within me there was something more to us then just friends yet I never wanted to over step the boundaries to what I might have interpreted as feelings and it was merely friendship." As he took her hand and kissed it she could feel the warmth of his breathe on her hand and the tenderness of his lips which conveyed to her that he was sincere in his intentions for establishing a relationship with her where completely honorable. As they entered the house everyone welcomed Kim with open arms their where three generations of Fredrick's family all under one roof laughing, talking, playing, and sharing remember when stories about times past. Then finally at the end of the long trail of relatives was his mother. She had a smile that could glow up a night sky and the skin the color of creamy caramel. Her hair was shoulder length and shinier than a new penny. She reached out her arms to embrace Kim and kissed her on the check. As Kim stood welcoming the warm embrace of Fredrick's mother she whispered in Kim's ear "baby you are a God send". Kim didn't know what his mother meant by those words but sooner then later she was going to find out. Then she felt a strong pair of hands grab her around the waist and whip her around; it was Fredrick's father Mr. Addison. "Hello lovely lady I am none other then the father of this here striking lad you call your boyfriend." "If he ever get out of line you let me know and I will take him down, cause I taught him better then that." After meeting his family and enjoying all the delicious food that had been prepared Kim kindly thanked Fredrick's family gave them all hugs and decided it was time to call it a night. "So did you enjoy yourself tonight?" "Yes I did and your folks have a beautiful home." "Thank you, most of those things you seen on the walls and inside of the cabinets are artifacts my mother and father brought back with them from Egypt." "So how long were they over there?"

About 10 years total their research and findings have been published in a book titled, *The Riches of the Night.* "Wow! That's deep." "Yeah they really enjoyed what they were doing and it has been really inspiring for our family how they were able to go to a foreign country and discover and do things that many people before them could not. I'm proud of them. So onto something I am interested in what are you planning to do with yourself for the rest of the evening?" "I don't know I hadn't really planned anything." "Why?" "I was just curious. Would you like to see the new place I'm looking into buying? It's one of those foreclosure properties that needs to be fixed up but with the money I am going to save during the purchase it will be worth it. So what do you say?"

"O.k., I guess it's still early." They drove down to 152nd Street and Florencedale the Street was well lit and each home on the block had a nice seven foot fence around it. The car slows to a crawling speed and stopped. "We are here;" Fredrick said as he put the car in park. He grabbed Kim by the hand and took her around to the side of the house where the realtor's box was located. Inside the box was a key. He opened the door and began to give Kim the grand tour. To her surprise the inside of the house was in really good shape. There were hard wood floors in every room and a dual fire place which was located between the living room and kitchen. The windows already had custom made casted iron bars on them and the home had a total of four rooms, two car garage, two baths, a study, kitchen, dining, and open foyer with vaulted 10 foot ceilings. "Like I said it needs a little fixing up but I can do it." "Fredrick this is beautiful." "I love it, it is very nice."

"I am glad you like it;" he said as he leaned in close staring into her eyes. "That was all the conformation I needed, this house is as good as sold." He took her by the hand and said; "let's go it's getting late and I need to get you home before your mother starts to worry about you." Kim smiled and said ok.

"If you wanted to know my name all you had to do was ask.

Running over to the window to find the missing past. Jumping to my feet or kneeling on my knees. Singing songs of praise. Praying for the day I want to see. Reading a word of wisdom to refresh the reason why. I am here looking up to heaven. Loving you all the same being afraid I hear your command. Run to use your spirit because it is within. Watching the masses on Sunday's inviting you in because of all that you have been. Seeking a better way to demonstrate the courage you have provided me I spend. Doing all that you could do only to be told it wasn't good enough. Wishing upon a star for a gift that really wasn't what you wanted at all. Depending on someone who told you no matter what they would always be there only to find out they were going to leave the minute you asked for help. Always giving your last depriving yourself of the best so that others may have only to find out the ones you gave all betrayed you and took more then what belonged. Giving your heart unselfishly to man who refused to spend the time it would take to turn a door knob to find out what really makes you happy. Searching for answers to truths which you already knew yet you needed confirmation to use as an excuse to why you stayed so long wondering about a future which you never thought time would bring never thinking you'd hear the love of your life call you another woman's name. Throwing a penny in a wishing well and believed in it more than God For as much as you have and all to which you have been through remember what is done is passed and all which is to be is up to you. What has started is a cycle that does not end with you for your bed is made; the game is through do unto others as you will have them do unto you.

"Hey girl what's up I haven't heard from you in a month of Sunday's where have you been?" "What have you been up to lately the girls and I were all worried about you?"

"I have been around just trying to figure out what to do with the rest of my life." Kim's friends were getting together for their weekend ritual. "You want to come with us it will be just like old times?" "Ok let me just check things over with Fredrick and I will call you later." "You two have really hit it off and now ya'll are acting like an old married couple." "Whatever!" "I will call you after my job interview tomorrow with my final decision." "Alright mother maid, ha ha ha," Stephanie taunts. "You are not even cute," Kim responds.

Rrrrring, rrrring, rrrring "What who could this be calling it's four O' clock in the morning?" "Hello? Who... awe, who is this," Kim said with a very sleepy voice?

"It's me, can I come over I need to talk?" "O.K" she said clearing her throat. "Is everything O.k.?" "Is your mom, dad, and Roger alright?" "Yeah baby I just need to talk to you." "It's o.k. I'm up." "Good because I'm outside your door." "What!" Fully awake now she jump to her feet and rushed to the bathroom to quickly brush her teeth and wash her face careful not to wake her mother and Kenny in the process. Tip toeing down the hall she crept to the front door. "Come in," she said in a very low whisper. "No I can't." "Can you step out for a minute?" "I promise I won't keep you long this is very important." "What is wrong, Fredrick you are scaring me?" "Sorry baby I just need to tell you something.

I am leaving tomorrow for a few weeks I have to take care of some business and I will be back but I didn't want to leave without telling you." "What?" "Why?" "Where are you going?" Her heart begin to pound she knew that if he were to walk out of her life again she wouldn't know if she would have the strength to wait for another seven years.

"I am going to finalize the purchase of the house and then I am going to take care of something in Davenport I will return in a few weeks." "Same old Fredrick," she says. "At least I didn't give you any of my precious temple this time before you decided to walk." "Baby please it's not like that this is very important I wish I could tell you more right now but I can't please just trust me I promise I will call you everyday." "O.k?" "I Love you baby and just know that I will be back in a couple of weeks." "O.k." Kim said as she looked at him with tearful eyes. "Awe baby please don't do this to me I am a man but I ain't above crying." "I don't ever want to see you hurting for no one not even me there is no man worth that but God." "I know," she said "I just, I just I love you Fredrick." He grabbed her by the small of her waist and kissed her lips ever so softly while holding the back of her neck pulling her closer as he started to rise up and take a stand she pulled away. "Baby we can't do this now." "I know he said, I 'm sorry I just lost control for a second." "I didn't mean to disrespect you; this is not what I came for." "You don't have to apologize." "I'll save myself for you!" "I'm proud of you. That's great!" "Why are you so excited, she asked?" "Huh nothing, I mean now I have no worries because no other man can try to steal you away from me while I am gone." He laughed as she looked at him with despising eyes. "I'm just kidding baby but I promise I will be back sooner then you think" "I will call you everyday." They shared another passionate kiss and said good night.

"Follow a path down to it's end to see where it will take you only to know that it is not taking you far enough for you to get through. You preach you practice you serve as a model of the life you lead only to find Learning how to deal with life all by myself. Playing a round of my favorite game all by myself. Hurting from a broken heart all by myself. Being alone in the dark all by myself.

Don't know where to go or who to turn to on the hardest day of my life all by myself. Waiting for a miracle all by myself."

Kim had a very strange way of dealing with her emotions. Everything in life seemed to have a story or some significant play of words she deemed poetic. Canted recaps of thoughts intertwined by the state of mental romance which she saw as an emotional unhinging to a noted past time. The next morning Kim woke up feeling as if she had won the lottery. As she crawled out of bed she felt a little different she looked down at her hand and there was a 4 carat Winston Herring Diamond engagement ring on her finger. She looked down on the night stand and there was a note written in really small script:

"Will you make me the happiest man in the world? Kimberly McMillan will you marry me?" "How could he?" "When did he;" she thought. "Ma!" "Maaaaaaaaaaaaa!" "What!" "Look, look at my hand." "Girl where did you get that?" "Ma you trying to tell me you had nothing to do with this?" "Girl I have no idea as to what you are talking about;" Mrs. McMillan stated as she walked over and hugged Kim with a big grin and said; "congratulations baby." For the remainder of the morning Kim could be heard throughout the house singing Brandi's rendition of *"Missing You"*. "Kim!" "Kim!" "Gurl what's wrong with you I have been calling you for two minutes in all I can here is this racket." "Who are you missing?" "Huh?" "No one ma, I just like that song." "O.k. yeah right, well let that there girl who gets paid to sing it sang the song until you leave my house today?" "I can't hear anything in here." "Yes ma'am," she said as she laughed her way to the kitchen. "Oh yeah before you go Fredrick called and said he will call you later around four O'clock." "He did?" "Mm huh like I'm crazy; ain't missing nobody my foot, gurl do you think I was born in a card board box?" "Alright ma me and the girls are going to go over to La La's I meant Lucy's house to hang out." "When Lucy bought a house?" "I

meant Mr. and Mrs. Fugal's house." "Alright baby you be careful out there on that road." "I will mama. I love you." "I Love you too baby." It was about one O' clock when Kim reached Stephanie's house. "What's up girl friend mmm huh you tell me you are the one with all the little well kept secrets huh whatcha talking about?" "You know what I am talking about you and Fredrick." "Oh well I didn't know if it was going any where so I just waited until I knew if it was going to be something." "Besides I knew Roger big mouth butt was going to tell you anyway." "Yeah but nevertheless you should have told me." "Ok so you going to be mad at me all day or what?" "Naw, I ain't mad; disappointed is all." "O.k yeah right, like the time you told us about the girl that was trying to creep with Roger that one time." "Oh that was different." "Yeah here you go with the double standards again." "Anyways, where are we going?" "Well everybody is supposed to meet up at Lucy's house and we are going out from there." "O.k let me grab my bag and I will be ready to go in about twenty seconds." "Oh let me say good bye to mom's and pop's so they don't go off." "I still can't believe that in a few months we will all be attending you and Fredrick's wedding." As promised Fredrick called everyday until he returned. Upon his return he explained to Kim that during his service in the Marine Corp. He witnessed some illegal code of ethics violations between two of his superiors which had to be kept confidential until after their trials. After sharing the news he explained to Kim that this is why he had to leave so suddenly and that he couldn't tell her for fear that someone would find out, then he too would be brought up on charges for leaking confidential government information. Upon his return Fredrick bought a small office in town and began his practice in the field of psychiatry almost immediately.

"The sunlight twinkles on the water like little flashing lights blinking rapidly for the attention of a day that is soon to pass. Incessant miles of Ocean elongated with an unperceived notion to carry a ship to its destination.

Cruising on a promise of relaxation to join together cultures of many different races. Burly and massive is the ocean so blue, clam, well respected and constantly traveled through. Willing to cooperate on a day when the weather causes perplexing emotions for an upset stomach. Finding treasures in a long narrow hall while walking pass strangers with big smiles. A lack of dedication and faith are covered with drinks to keep up the spirits with friends of varies attitudes. Suffering all alone because your pain is brushed with fear. Money well spent to travel to a different country while cruising on a ship."

Kim loved Fredrick so much but she was afraid she had not told him that she was keeping a very hurtful secret buried deep inside. But she figure that he would understand, so she made up in her mind that she was going to tell him tonight. The anticipation was increasingly growing inside of her. Instead of waiting until that night she figured she would drive over to his office and surprise him and get the full experience of lying on his big leather couch and experiencing what the rest of his patients experienced. She arrived at Fredrick's office and she waited patiently outside until he was finished. Kim had signed in as a patient and was waiting to be treated as such. Fredrick opened the door without looking out into the waiting room he looked at the name on the list with a puzzled look aaahhh "Mrs. Addison" expecting to see his mother, as Kim stood to her feet. "Oh baby you know you didn't have to sign in to see me, come in." "Debra please hold all calls and visitors until further notice." "Yes Sir, Debra responded." "What's up baby?"

Kim lay down on the leather couch and said, "Baby I have something to tell you." "Ok," Fredrick responded. "I …I… I" Kim sat up on the couch with tears streaming down her cheeks and begins to pour out all the details about the night she vowed to never relive. During her third year of college on the way to her dorm from the library Kim had been sexually assaulted by an unsuspecting person. She explained that she had been dating a very nice young man named Mike who was the casting director for the Art intern program. He called her earlier that evening to break off a date he had with her. She told him that she would then go to the library and get some studying done. On her way back from the library she took a route she most commonly used to short cut her way to her dorm in 10 minutes. Although it was still earlier many of the people who were normally out that night had went home for the Labor Day holiday weekend. She explained right before the attack she remembered feeling a sharp pain in her lower back and she blacked out. When she came to she could smell the fragrance of English Leather cologne and alcohol. Her assailant had restrained her legs with shoe laces as she struggled to get free. He promptly punched her in the face twice with two solid blows to her nose and mouth as she begged him to release her. She screamed with fear as the pain of the blows rushed to her face. She cried out for help praying that anyone would hear her as her attacker then placed a dirty sock in her mouth. Her hands were securely bound behind her back as she wiggle around like a fish out of water trying to keep him from violating her. This only made him angrier as he grabbed her a begin ripping her clothing from her body. A slither of light trickled through the trees allowing her to see overhead. The area was unfamiliar to her and she realized that she was no longer on the college campus and that her attacker must have carried or drove her away after knocking her unconscious. With terror in her eyes she thought to herself God please let this be a dream. She soon felt the gut wrenching pain of her attacker violating her physical rights. He was very violent in the manner of his attack brutally forcing himself inside of her in leadership and follow-up positions repeatedly for 2 hours. Kim felt as if some one hand taken sand paper in rubbed and scraped her insides out. Upon completion of this attack he stood over her and laughed as he proceed to soak her with discarded remnants of alcohol while she lay in the fetal position crying like an abandon infant. Crying hysterically at this point she continued on explaining to Fredrick that he then cut off the restraints and just walked away into the night leaving her to find her way back to the main highway and walk the 4 miles back to the campus scared and humiliated. She remembers returning to her dorm trying to wash off the stench of the attack. She refused to share her horrific ordeal with anyone including Mike. She was too embarrassed to call the police in report the incident and too afraid. She withdrew from Mike and looked at him with such terror and fear any time he tried to show any signs of affection. She became very withdrawn, broke off her relationship with Mike and decided to check herself into a mental hospital for suicidal victims. She then begins to tell Fredrick how she promptly left the college and moved 300 miles away without telling anyone. She had a desire to finish college and she switched her major and earned a degree in criminal justice. She had never shared her story with anyone to this date other then him. As she fell to her knees on the floor Fredrick knelt down next to her holding her face in his hands looking in her eyes he says; "for every man in life that has hurt you I'm sorry baby, but I will never let anyone hurt you ever again." As she shakes her head in agreement she says; "that's not the worst of it." "I later got the courage to seek help and I went to see a doctor after feeling sick and weak." After running test it was discovered that I was 3 weeks pregnant." "To make matters worst I am under observation for HIV testing." "Wow, Fredrick says." Fredrick stood looking lost and disbelief. "So what happened?" "I mean, like do you have a child?" "No;" she stated, "I aborted the child." "No child deserved to live a life such as that." "Baby I am here for you and we can do this together, O.K.?" "O.K" "I Love you." "I love you too Fredrick."

Beep, beep, beep, beep, beep, beep.

The closer the date for her last sixth month testing was soon upon Kim and she became more frighten. The pain from not knowing was literally killing her.

CHAPTER 6

K IM walks into Fredrick's office and says; "what would you do if you found out I was HIV positive?" "What?" "I just want to know what you would do if the test comes back and shows that I am HIV positive." "How are you going to react; do you think you would leave me?" "Absolutely," he says. Then he laughed and grabbed her by the face saying I'm just kidding you know I love you; you mean the world to me I am going to be here for you. Kim waited in the lounge praying to God for strength that only he could provided to get her through the anticipation of waiting to find out the ultimate truth of whether or not she would live her life with the deadly disease that was killing thousands of young African Americans every year. "Good morning Kim the doctor will see you now." It seemed like forever before Kim approached the door she slowly turned the knob and took a deep breathe. "Well hello Ms. McMillan it is good seeing you again." "So how have you been feeling lately?" "Ok I guess." "Doc if you don't mind I would like to cut past the small talk and find out the results of my test." Although those were the words that came out of Kim's mouth she really didn't mean it. If fact she was quite frightened and the anticipation of not knowing the result clouded her mind into speaking. "O.k. then, I completely understand." "I must say though before I reveal the results regardless of the outcome your life is precious at any state and is worth living and you have plenty of options as far as help for getting through the aftermath." "Yes sir she responded." "Your test results reveal....," Kim sat down in the chair crying becoming overwhelmed with emotion Dr. Floyd enters the room. "Kim I realize that you have a lot to deal with right now and if you want I can set up an appointment to see a psychiatrist friend of mine she is really good." "No thanks." "Well the results have revealed that you are all clear." "You did not contract Aids nor the HIV virus strand of Aids, congratulations!" "I do hope that you will seek professional help for dealing with your mental afflictions." "Thank you so very much Doc." "May I have a copy of my results?" "Sure stop by the front desk on your way out and ask Shirley for a copy." Kim gladly celebrated her results with Fredrick. They were soon married shortly there after and they moved into their new home. Fredrick became very productive at his psychiatry office and Kim was preparing to make partner at one of the most well known firms in town. In spite of the buzz flying around the office Kim kept her guard up and continued to work just as hard on every case. She was very dedicated to her job and to her husband. She was always home by five O' clock to prepare a hot meal. After all that she had been through her life finally begin to feel complete. She and Fredrick were planning to establish a nice six figure nest egg before having children and they were very close to their quota estimating another year or so before they would settle. It was a Friday afternoon and Kim was just rapping up with her last client getting ready to head home when she got this sharp pain in her hip. "Whoa!" "Are you ok Mrs. Addison," asked Mr. Malika the door man as he opened the door to let her out. "Yes, Mr. Malika could you please have the valet pull my car around?" "Yes ma'am

Mrs. Addison." "Ouch;" she yelled as he quickly turned to assist her. "Are you sure you are alright?" "Mmmmm I think so, it's probably just stress." "I will soak in the tub and try to relax when I get home." "Thank you Mr. Malika, have a good weekend, you too Mrs. Addison." That afternoon Fredrick arrived home looking very tired. Kim was standing in the kitchen preparing a nice candlelit dinner. "Hey baby, are you ready for dinner or would you like to shower first?"

"Give me a minute baby I'm gonna go shower and then I will meet you at the table in 15 minutes." "O.K," Kim senses a distant and withdrawn vibe coming from Fredrick. She turned the stove off and proceeded to enter the bedroom when she heard him talking on the telephone. "You know what I can't deal with this right now!" "I told you before stop calling me when I am home!" "You should have taken care of that situation four months ago!" With a puzzled look on her face Kim pushed open the door. "Is everything O.K baby." "Huh?" "Uh, yeah just a client wanting to know if they could schedule an appointment last minute." He grabbed her around the waist and kissed her then slowly and seductively making a trail from her chin down her neck to her shoulder and gently nibbling her neck while slowly sucking blood to the surface of her skin. "You know people at the office will talk if I walk in with a hicky on my neck." "I don't care about them people you are my wife, maybe if the were getting some on the regular they wouldn't be worried about you," he said. Pushing her slowly towards the bed and delicately unbuttoning her shirt. Just as the phone rang "ignore it," he whispered in her ear. She flip open his phone and saw the name Heather she quickly closed it and mentioned that the food was getting cold as she pushed him off of her. "O.k I see how you are." "You won't even let me grind on you huh?" "Hurry up beside your boys, the ladies, and we are supposed to go out tonight." "Naw baby ya'll go ahead I'm in for the night." "I got a busy day schedule for tomorrow." "What!" "Tomorrow is the weekend and the office is closed." "Come on baby I just have a few files that Debra forgot to put vital information in, so I have to straighten them out to make sure it is done correctly this time." "It's not her fault we got this new system we..." Just then the phone rang again. As Kim walked over to pick it up she could see the name Heather flash on the caller I.D as Fredrick reached over to mash the receiver. "Why did you hang up the phone?" "It is after hour's baby I don't have time for all that nonsense." "You go hang out have a nice time and tell them I will catch them on the rebound."

It was at that moment that Kim's woman's intuition kicked in and she decided to concoct a plan to prove her heart felt theory. "If he is cheating what am I going to do," she thought? "I will wait until she calls again and I will confront her first maybe she doesn't even know he is married." It had been six weeks since the Heather phone calls and Kim began to assume that she in fact had over reacted. The phone rang Kim looked at the caller I.D and it was Stephanie. "Hey girl what's up?" "Nothing much what are you doing?" "I need your help real quick how fast can you get to the Smart Mart on 87th Ave about two minutes?" "Why?" "Girl I got a flat tire and I need a lift hurry up, you know people down here are a trip about leaving your vehicle." "O.K I'm on my way." Kim pulled in the parking lot to see Stephanie sitting inside her car parked in the back in the shadows sitting low under the steering wheel. "Girl you better have a flat tire somewhere on this car or I'm gonna flat one for you making me drive over here for nothing." Just then Stephanie says nothing and just points in the west direction across the street where Fredrick was standing with a little boy about four years old that look so much like him you would think that he gave birth himself. There was a woman sitting inside the car with the word Heather on the windshield. Kim's heart begins to pound so hard and heavy you would think it was literally going to beat out of her chest. She had to keep her cool because she did not want to make a scene. Filled with angry, confusion, and hurt she headed for home to call Fredrick to see what his excuse would be for his whereabouts. Upon arriving home she picked up the phone to dial his number as he was walking through the door. Before she could hear the second ring she heard the key in the door. "Hey baby how was your day?" "Great how was yours?" She pretended to be excited as usual to see him it took every thing she had in her to keep the smile plastered on her face. "Good in spite of all the traffic," stated Fredrick. "So did you get off a little later then normal today or did you stop off somewhere?"

"Yeah I got off late and I stopped by my home boy's house for a minute to see if he was home." "Why didn't you just call him on the phone?" "What's with all the questions Inspector Gadget?" "Nothing I was just curious." "I know you are normally home by now I was a little worried that's all." "Well I'm here baby, I ain't going no where."

"I have a surprise for you as she slowly unbuttons the top of her shirt." "Are you serious?" "Yeah, I'm going to go take a shower and I'll be right back." "O.k. I'm going to go pour us something to drink." Fredrick walks to the kitchen as Kim quickly grabs his cell phone from his coat pocket she goes into the bathroom and press redial. The phone rings on the second ring a woman answers; "hello baby are you calling to tell your son good night?" "Hold on"; a small voice on the other end says, "hello daddy?"

Kim quickly hangs up the phone. It begins to ring as she turns the phone off and tosses it on the bed. Kim hears Fredrick's footsteps coming down the hall. She runs to the bathroom and begins to cry silently into a towel to muffle the sound as she shakes uncontrollably. Thinking to her self how could he do this? Kim decides she was not going out without a fight and the most vindictive revenge for his wicked ways of indiscretion would be the ultimate payback of her own. As she showers Kim thinks of a way to carry out her plan without causing further hurt to her self. Then it hit her, she remembered hearing about a woman who used super glue to teach her husband a lesson. Kim thought about this plan as her a sufficient plan for her payback to Fredrick for the pain and the hurt of his discretions. As she prepared for the moment she laced her skin with sweet scents of Intention and hot oils. She glossed her lips with Victoria secret strawberry lip gloss the kind that actually tasted like strawberries when she licked her lips. She then put on her two piece black open cut Victorian laced negligee with matching black stiletto pumps. She walked into the shadows of candlelight reaching for the play button on the stereo the music begins playing a slow mix of *Gerald Levert, R Kelly* and *Keith Sweat.* She danced slow and seductive bending over; touching her toes and moving just right allowing the silhouettes to cast traces of her body on the wall. She moved in closer and closer to Fredrick's body until she could feel her skin rubbing against him. She gave him a nice slow lap dance allowing him to trace her zenith of her breast with his tongue as she grabbed his head shoving it forcefully into the pit of her bosom. She rose up and down cradling his head then she bent back his neck and lick a trail down to his six pack abs where she began to unbutton his pants with her teeth breathing heavily the warmth of her breath hitting his skin with every pull then she started up again as she pulled down his pants then lifting his shirt she made another trail down to his navel from his neck stopping occasionally to suck on his skin. Fredrick was fully erect and gripping the sheets of the bed trembling as if he was being electrocuted by a hot wire. He released the covers and grabbed her hair slowly pushing her down to face his manhood. She opened his thighs and trace her wet soft tongue along his inter thigh meanwhile slowly uncapping the super glue she began dripping it's entire contents on to him and pushing his triton which stood at full staff onto his leg with her stiletto heel as she yelled "it's over you bastard!" For every incident in life Kim seemed to use poetic expression to help her rationalize her thoughts:

"Giving all you have until you have nothing for your self in the end you are not a statistic you are just giving all that you can close your eyes and wonder if what you do can make a difference wading in water that only you can see as you're blinking one eye fast. Looking for a place to go when the shelters wont let you in cast out to the world to live the best you can scratching for food to feed a family that is beyond the help and need looking to the ones you trust most only to be deceived your blinking one eye fast.

I watched him form across the room with the deep stare in his eyes the look he had when we first met him the one that was hard to bare he could make me drop to my knees by simply caressing my face and smelling my hair. He would hold my body close and squeezing an in just the right place. When he loved me with his mind it became more powerful then his heart could every erase. If he took me out on a date everyone would watch because I was the only woman in town that couldn't be replaced. I was his favorite flower and I knew it when he smiled for it would last for days and thought s of me drove him wild. He was my first true love and I his soul mate A life of dedications and years of love on a plate Master minds couldn't break his spirits nothing negative said was ever true No lies, no fields of compromise would ever damage or taint images of me As time passed on I looked across the room I found a look in the eyes of the man I thought I knew only to find he wasn't looking at me with tearful eyes I continued to be the graceful woman who I'd always be I walked over and softly whisper in his ear it's better to live your life with a woman who loves you I lived life with you in my heart under lock in key all this hurts to see you love, but it was better when you loved me."

"Courageous little infants defy the odds of life; fight for the will to live to make their presence known as a mother willfully makes a choice to end her very own. Where is hope? Top of the class her parents were so proud until the day the gun shot rung out to deliver the black cloud. Successful and smart she was a partner at her firm until the day she forgot to lock her car door not knowing this one fatal mistake and she would not make it home. Where is the hope? Ten children playing hop scotch on a neighborhood street seven shot dead by a drive by shooting miraculously sparing three. A wife holding on to a cheating husband for the sake of her kids only to find that in four years and treatments later her life would still end. Where is the hope?"

CHAPTER 7

"OK I will see you around 2:30 at Calvarias Italian restaurant on the corner of 23rd and Broadway." "O.k. baby I will see you then," her mother responded. Kim really desired to get help for all the pit falls she was having about her and Fredrick's relationship so she decided to speak with her mother during lunch. "Good afternoon ladies my name is Mason I am going to be your waiter this afternoon may I start you with some thing to drink?" "Yes, I will have a sweet ice tea with lemon please." "Make that two, Mrs. McMillan responded" "That's easy enough, I will be right back with your drink orders, take your time look over the menus, and if you have any questions feel to ask." "Honey what's wrong you sounded so worried over the phone is everything ok with you and Fredrick?" "No ma'am. I left him he has been seeing another woman that he has a four year old son with." "What!" "You heard me right," Kim responded. " "I don't know what to do about it?" "I feel like my whole like I have been walking around on padded shoes trying to please everyone else and I continue to get hurt in the process. It's like walking softly on padded shoes so know one will hear, a sound from you guiding yourself softly across the land, playing songs of romance for mildly men. Rigors of long days standing on pins while justice for others lives are of suspense. Quietness as a demand not as a request. Others are treated like the best. Being just a spot on a page without significant time. Meanwhile front rows for all as I stand in line. Scraps left on the table after everyone else gets done eating the best minion. Scrap it up. Pitch it out. What's left is for you. This is the life of a taken for granted wife walking softly on padded shoes." "O.K baby I know you are hurting but have you talked to Fredrick and discussed with him what is really going on?" "Why ma I'm like the man who was fishing in the desert." "A man was in the desert for 40 days with his hook he return to the city to tell all he knew about how he caught a snook. Look down in my boat he said; "I would like for you to see". All the people laugh because they didn't notice anything. The man said; "no it's there look really hard, can't you see?" The people begin to laugh again and said you must be mistaken. When the man look down he saw the fish shaking in the boat. Why can't you see the fish? He said; it's so big it is impossible not to see.I caught him in the desert it was astonishing to me. The man looked down again and this time the fish spoke. It is not always easy for others to see that which is clearly obvious unless it makes sense. Because they knew you were in the desert they did not believe and their vision became clouded with judgment before they could ever see." "Come on now I know you use poetry as part of your healing process yet I also think you use it as a means to escape from the real world." "Baby you need to take it to the Lord and give it unto him." Upon the advice of her mother she decided to seek help from the source that was higher then any other. Kim went to church that Sunday morning to not only recommit her life to Christ but to also release all of the devastating issues about her life to the only one willing force who could take on her life's struggles. After the sermon the door of the church were opened for all those who were willing to come onto Jesus for rest. Some where in between asking for prayer and confessing her problems to the pastor Kim had been noted kneeling for a period of eight minutes before she was then shaken and awaken by her mother with tear streaked cheeks and a host of her Christian peers. She had willfully confessed an entire life of terror that would never be forgotten. Kim had been raped, she never completely got over her father's death and the one person she had fallen in love with betrayed her. Because of her mental state of destruction she decided she thought she was no longer fit to live. Kim finally decided she was going to make choices about her own life and no one would ever hurt her again. Later that day she decided to check into a hotel because she couldn't face Fredrick or her mother. Rrrring... rrrring, "Hello?" "Hello Mrs. McMillan have you seen Kim I need to talk to her?" "Why haven't you hurt her enough?" "Listen Fredrick I don't normally get into ya'll business but I think right is right and wrong is wrong!" "You had no right to lead my daughter on and marry her if you knew you were still going to play the field."

"Hold on Mrs. McMillan let me explain, Heather is not nor have she ever been my girlfriend." "I just recently found out I was adopted and I was raised by the Addison's as their own child." "It wasn't until I was in the Marine Corp that I learned about my twin brother we were separated at birth and he was recently killed in the line of duty." "When I found out he had a wife and a kid I went down to meet them and pay my respects." "When I went to Heather's house she explained to me that she didn't have the nerve to tell their four year old son his father was dead." "When he saw my face he immediately assumed I was his father because we were identical." "She begged me to play along until she could find the time to tell him." "I initially agreed and we just pretended I was my brother and I went back to the Marine Corp so the kid wouldn't know the difference but when she followed me here she crossed the line." "I never told Kim about it because she was already dealing with some difficult situations from her past." "What are you talking about Fredrick," she asked? "I will let her tell you." "Please Mrs. McMillan do you know where she is?" "No son, sorry I don't." Kim enter the hotel room lit a candle, chanted a solemn prayer as she took a sip of water and lie down in the bed. She closed her eyes, her breathe became very shallow twenty-four pills and ten minutes later she was dead. The next morning her body was discovered by the housekeeper. The medical examiner shared the results of her autopsy with her mother and Fredrick. "I am sorry to inform you that she died from an overdose of over the counter sleeping pills and the baby did not survive." "What you mean she was....?" "Oh God no!"

"I'm sorry she was four months pregnant."